I0731388

Where Dreams Live

By Anne Dupré

Copyright © 2022 Anne Dupré

All rights reserved. No part of this book may be reproduced or transmitted in any form or by any means electronic or mechanical including photocopying, recording, or by any information storage and retrieval system without permission in writing from the publisher.

Aurora Books, an imprint of Eco-Justice Press, L.L.C.

Aurora Books
P.O. Box 5409 Eugene, OR 97405
www.ecojusticepress.com

Where Dreams Live
by Anne Dupré

Library of Congress Control Number: 2021949486
ISBN 978-1-945432-49-1

For all who have a dream

Table of Contents

What happened in the past is lived again in memory. To revive it is to enhance the present moment with new meaning. Only then do the details compose into a story.

John Dewey

I'm Going to Be a Ballerina

When I leaped out of bed, dawn was still waiting for the day to begin. I pressed my face to the window, my breath fogging the pane. Through the mist, I could see the empty stone urns had already formed snow mountains high enough for the squirrels to slide down, and the snow continued falling. If it had snowed the day before, I would have run out after breakfast to make a snowman, but that day each flake, lovely and light, fell to the ground with disappointment. I ran to the kitchen.

"Good morning, Sarah. You're up early. I'm making your favorite. Sit down and have some waffles with strawberries and whipped cream."

"We're still going, Mommy, aren't we? We're still going. Right?"

"We'll see, Sarah." Mom turned to the window and shook her head.

"We have to go, Mommy. We have to go."

"We'll see."

Dad walked to the window and sighed. "Not a great day to drive to the city, is it, Sarah?"

"Daddy, we have to go." I slumped in the chair and watched the cream on my waffle turn pink as it melted into the warm strawberry sauce.

"Sarah, please eat your waffle."

"I'm not hungry." I ran to the front door, my fingers crossed. The driveway was already covered with a foot of snow, the wind forming drifts that could reach to my chin, and the snow had no pity. It just kept falling. I ran back to Dad.

"Daddy, we have to go. We have to go, Daddy."

Dad ate his waffles quickly and winked on his way to get his parker. "Let's see what I can do, Sarah." I ran up and wrapped my arms around him.

As I watched Dad from the window, I leaped up and down with every shovelful he tossed to the wind. Soon the sun shone bright and the wind became gentle and the heavy snowflakes turned to flurries. I could see Dad clearly now. He was smiling and gave me a thumbs up. We were going to the *Nutcracker Ballet,* Aunt May's Christmas gift for her girl with dancing feet.

For as long as I can remember I wanted to be a ballerina. In an early memory I'm drifting off to sleep to the sound of the wind chime swaying on a branch of the kwanzan tree and dreaming my special dream.

In a pine forest
Filled with candied sweets and crystal snowflakes,
A little ballerina dances to the delicate ringing of bells.

I returned to this dream often. The little ballerina and I had become great friends, and Aunt May's Christmas gift that year brought me to the place where my dream lived.

We left around noon. As we drove through town, the sun smiled on the snow topped limbs of every tree, and the highway was clear. But when we exited the tunnel, the city didn't care that we were going to the ballet. The traffic was heavy, and crowds of people gathered on every corner. As they hurried to cross the streets, sometimes ignoring the lights, the honking horns demanding to be heard got no attention at all.

I wouldn't allow the city clamor to intrude on the Sugar Plum Fairy dancing in my head. Embracing the pink ballet slippers Aunt May gave me brought me to a quiet place. "If you wear the magic slippers when you twirl around your room with your willow hoop dream-catcher, Dancing Feet, your ballerina dream will come true," my aunt had said. I wore the ballet slippers during the whole ballet.

The auditorium buzzed with a good excitement. Children in their holiday best were finding it hard to behave. Some ran down the aisles to peer into the orchestra pit. Others skipped around holding hands with their friends. When I took off my boots and put on my ballet slippers, something magical happened. My "happy" feet refused to be still, and I started dancing in the aisle.

"Sarah, please come and sit down now."

The lights dimmed and the hall settled down. The memory is as vivid as if it were happening now.

The gold curtain rises on the eve of Christmas over 100 years ago. In the drawing room Mother and Father are trimming a tall fir tree. Marie and her brother Fritz are napping. A moonbeam shining through the window casts a silver light on the wooden owl flapping its wings on top of the grandfather clock. "It's time. It's time. It's time for the party to begin."

Marie and her brother wake up and run to the drawing room. Father is placing the last ornament on the giant green pine, radiant in the candle light, and beckons the children in. It's the grandest tree they've ever seen. Gingerbread snowmen and candied canes and crystal stars hang from every limb. Presents in shiny gold paper and big silk bows wait under the tree to bring joy to everyone.

Soon uncles and aunts and so many cousins arrive splendidly dressed. The young ladies in long dresses with matching satin bows in their hair. The boys in fine velvet jackets and long pants. Filled with the spirit of the season and the magic of candlelight, the girls dance merrily around the glittering tree, and the boys jump over each other's backs in a frisky game of leapfrog.

Suddenly an old man wrapped in a black cloak and wearing a black patch over one eye whirls in like a blustery gust of wind. When he opens his cape, he looks like a giant black bird with wings, but the children aren't afraid. It's Godfather Drosselmeyer. Many magical things happen when he comes to visit.

This evening Godfather Drosselmeyer arrives with his handsome nephew and three large boxes filled with surprises. The children gather round as Godfather D lifts out life-sized dolls and winds them up. A harlequin in a diamond pattern suit comes to life and dances with his beloved Columbine. A soldier with a fine feathered plume rising high on his head springs up, shoots his rifle, bends down on one knee, and gives a sassy salute.

There are special gifts, too. Like the ballerinas dancing in the goodnight parades in my dreams, the little ladies cradle their porcelain dolls in fancy silk dresses and sashay around the tree. The boys blow their shiny gold bugles and bang their red drums in a snappy military march, and the hobby horse they all want to ride causes a fierce tug of war.

But Marie receives the best gift of all. "Look, Mommy," I whisper. "Marie has a nutcracker cavalier just like the one Aunt May gave me."

"Grandma bought Aunt May the cavalier on the day she attended the ballet when she was your age," Mom whispers. Even at five years old I understood the bond my aunt and I had.

Standing off to the side, the cavalier held gently in her arms, Marie watches the rowdy boys banging their drums and stamping their feet. In a reckless gesture her high-spirited brother sweeps by, snatches the wooden soldier, throws it to the floor, and stomps on his head.

Godfather Drosselmeyer rescues the nutcracker and gives the cavalier back to Marie with his jaw wrapped in a handkerchief. She presses the injured nutcracker close to her heart, and her Godfather's handsome nephew gives her a little bed for the wounded cavalier. Marie likes the gentle boy very much. As he leads the girls and boys in a minuet, he dances like a prince.

At the end of the night when Marie and the handsome boy say goodbye, I remember hoping they would meet again. Maybe Marie will even dream about him, I think. I always dream about things I wish will come true.

Marie and Fritz go to their beds. The only sound's the owl on top of the grandfather clock announcing the midnight hour. Marie tip-toes back to the drawing room to get her nutcracker. Cradling the cavalier in her arms, she curls up on the couch and falls asleep.

A wind passes through the open window, the curtains billow, and the magic begins --

MARIE ENTERS THE ENCHANTING WORLD WHERE DREAMS LIVE.

Watching the tree tremble and grow to an enormous height takes my breath away, but when the nutcracker grows as tall as Marie, I spring to my feet. Even with his large head and wide mouth, the cavalier looks handsome in his blue and red uniform. He has gold epaulets on each shoulder and a silver-hilted sword by his side just like my nutcracker cavalier.

"Please sit down, Sarah," Dad whispers.

In a flash an army of mice sweep across the darkened stage, and a mouse as big as a bear darts out of the dark. Two ugly teeth protrude from each of his several heads which are topped with tiny gold crowns. The giant mouse charges towards the nutcracker. A fierce battle ensues, and the cavalier runs his silver saber through the evil mouse-king's heart. Released from the ancient spell that has given him a large head and wide, grinning mouth, the nutcracker changes into a stately prince and looks very much like Godfather Drosselmeyer's handsome nephew.

Then soaring up to the sky in a magical sleigh, Marie and her prince come to an enchanting pine forest nestled in the glow of moonlight. At the edge of the forest ballerinas in silvery-white tutus dance like delicate flakes of snow

"How beautiful, Mommy." Mom nods and puts her finger to her lips.

Their hearts joined in joy, Marie and the prince follow the Christmas star to the magical realm of the Sugar Plum Fairy. A cloud lifts, and the Sugar Plum Fairy, attended by angels with halos and gold wings, dances to the gentle ringing of bells, her pink tutu speckled with glimmering jewels. My eyes open wide. The ballerina looks very much like the Sugar Plum Fairy pirouetting in my dreams.

With a wave of her hand, the Sugar Plum Fairy welcomes Marie and the prince to delicacies from around the world. Chocolates from Spain dance to the spirited music of trumpets and castanets. Pink and yellow marzipan step nimbly waving their gold pan flutes, and candy canes in red and green stripes jump sprightly through big round hoops.

And so much more. Cherry-cheeked cherubs burst from

Mother Ginger's huge hoop skirt. The girls curtsy and the boys bow before springing into a lively dance. When the children return beneath the billowing skirt, Mother Ginger waves enthusiastically as she exits the stage. The audience cheers.

"Mommy, I just love the ballet." Mom kisses my cheek. "So do I, Sarah."

In the quiet that follows, ballerinas, a perfect bouquet of pink blossoms, unfurl in a glorious waltz. A dewdrop glimmering in the glow of the moon's light bounds upon the stage brushing the tip of each bloom. The Waltz of the Flowers is so lovely I wish Isabella could be here. My little pug loved dancing to the *Nutcracker Suite.*

Then accompanied by the enchantment of harps, the Sugar Plum Fairy dances a grand pas de deux with her cavalier. Her pirouettes and grands je-tés end in a heart-stopping dive into her handsome prince's arms.

"Brava. Brava."

But even dreams must come to an end. Soaring off in their magical sleigh pulled by four-wingéd reindeer, Marie and her prince bid farewell. Flying to where the moon meets the sun, they arrive at Christmas morning.

Although I wasn't happy to see the ballet end, dreams are made from moments like this, and that night I fell asleep to the sound of bells and the Sugar Plum Fairy dancing in my head.

In an enchanted forest in the moonlight,
And the sound of bells ringing everywhere,
A beautiful ballerina pirouettes lighter than air
In the arms of her cavalier.

When I woke up Christmas morning, the dream was still real. As I twirled around the kitchen waving my willow hoop dream-catcher, I announced with absolute determination, **"Mommy, I'm gonna to be a ballerina someday!"**

Mom said I had been springing into the air since I took my first wobbly step. I could turn round like the wheels of a bicycle across the school playground for my friends. Even Terry whose legs were long and lean couldn't do a cartwheel, and hanging upside down on the top rung of the monkey bars, my long brown hair sweeping the ground, didn't scare me at all.

"Sarah, be careful. You're gonna fall." Patty thought climbing was a reckless thing to do, and she always stood by ready to catch me if I fell. She was a very good friend.

I remember the night the snow fell quietly and one star illuminated the sky. I made a wish: "Star light, star bright, please teach me to dance tonight." When I drifted off to sleep to the sound of the wind chime, I had a wonderful dream.

Beneath trees with snow-rimmed limbs
Glistening in the light of the moon,
A little ballerina dances like the wind.

At the first light of day, I leaped out of bed and bound around my room accompanied by the sweet melody of two red-breasted robins in the kwanzan tree. I wanted more than anything in the world to be that ballerina dancing like the wind.

The Christmas Aunt May gave me a CD of the *Nutcracker Ballet* and her very own nutcracker cavalier with a large head and wide mouth which I thought handsome anyway, I began living the dream. Twirling around the living room with the cavalier close to my heart, the flickering lights on our Christmas tree joining the fun, I felt as glorious as the Sugar Plum Fairy.

In spring and summer, the grass green and lush, my cavalier and I whirled tirelessly across my wide-spreading lawn. Even over yellow and crimson leaves or on cold blustery days, with the wind sending the scent of pine to sweeten the earthy smell of dry leaves, I loved dancing with my cavalier held tightly in my arms.

Then my real live dancing partner came to live with us. It was a Friday in June. I had just arrived home from nursery school when Dad pulled into the driveway with that special look in his eyes.

"Come see what I have, Sarah."

Dad placed Isabella, no bigger than his hand, gently in my arms. The red bow around her neck was almost as big as she was. "Oh Daddy, she's so cute. Look at her curly tail and monkey face." Holding the little pug close to my heart, we danced our first pas de deux. Aunt May had already begun teaching me ballet terms, and I started using the French words all the time. I thought they sounded magical.

Every morning, the roses in full bloom bordering the patio and the butterflies flying up to kiss the sun, Isabella and I twirled across the lawn. On rainy days we danced in my room to the music of the *Nutcracker* and the pitter patter of raindrops on the window pane.

"Up. Up. Jeté. Good girl, Iz."

Yes, Isabella was a dancer. At barely a year old she could leap higher than any pug I knew. Even Terry's Springer spaniel couldn't jump as high, but Teddy was only two months old then.

When I thought Isabella was ready for her first ballet performance, I invited Aunt May. With the sun peeking through the kwanzan leaves speckling her coat of fur gold, Isabella Ballerina leaped up high to get her stuffed monkey Max I held over her head.

"Brava, Isabella Ballerina, Brava," Aunt May applauded. "Super jeté, little girl."

With her head held high and that special twinkle in her eyes, Izzie walked in triumph over to my aunt. Dropping the trophy from her mouth, she sprang up and gave Aunt May a great big lollypop-kiss.

The limelight suited Isabella Ballerina so well, and she was a great dancing partner. Our best pas de deux usually began after dark. When the lamplight outside my bedroom window cast weird and gigantic shadows on the wall, I knew they weren't dangerous, but I was still afraid. I always put on the *Nutcracker* to scare the ghosts away.

On the opening note Isabella Ballerina would leap from her bed and dash in between and around my legs. Her barks were in perfect harmony with the beautiful music, and the moon shining through the window spotlighted our dazzling duet.

"Up. Up. Jeté. Good girl, Iz."

"Sarah, please go to sleep now. Growing girls and puppies need their proper rest," Mom would call from the kitchen, but Tchaikovsky's music had cast its spell.

Yes, Isabella kept my ballerina dream alive, but the day Dad said the magic words "Brava, Dancing Feet. Brava," I knew my dream was going to come true.

The snow had fallen all through the night, forming valleys and hills across the lawn, and the patio table looked like a two-foot-high frosted cake. In the morning sun, the limbs of every tree and all the rhododendron bushes wore their glimmering coats of white proudly, and I was a happy little girl.

"Mommy, can Isabella and I go out and play in the snow?"

"Sure, Cupcake. Let's dress you up warmly." Mom tied the hood of my snowsuit tightly under my chin, wrapped a big woolen scarf around my neck, and gave me my warmest mittens to wear.

"Come on Iz. Let's go out and play in the snow." When I opened the back door, the cold wind whipped across Isabella's face. Taking her firm straight-legged stance, the folds in her wrinkled brow really noticeable, she refused to put even one paw in the snow. She never liked the cold and certainly didn't like getting her feet wet. And so sitting snug on her cushioned chair in the warm, cozy kitchen, she watched me from the window with that special twinkle in her big brown eyes.

I can still feel the cold air biting my face and my body tingling that day. With boots high to my knees, I surged across the lawn blanketed in snow to my waist. Cocooned in my hooded snowsuit and unwieldy boots, I leaped across snow mounds created by the wind as nimbly as a squirrel jumps from tree to tree.

As I propelled myself over the snowdrifts, Dad waved from the window and clapped his hands. "Brava, Dancing Feet. Brava." Even muffled through the pane of glass, Dad's words resounded. **I'm a dancer.**

As the clouds drifted across the sky and the temperature dropped, I swept into the house all breathless and rosy-cheeked. Looking as if I had just arrived from the arctic tundra, my cheeks stinging from the penetrating wind, I announced with absolute determination, **"Daddy, I'm going to be a ballerina someday!"**

"OK, Dancing Feet." Dad wiggled his nose across my nose like an Eskimo, whipped off my mittens, and rubbed my hands toasty. When I pulled off my boots and socks, Isabella licked my toes with her warm tongue.

"Daddy, let's make some cocoa." Then holding my little pug up by her front paws, we danced around the kitchen table. "Look, Daddy, Isabella wants to be a ballerina, too." With one turn and one leap into the air, Isabella Ballerina and I delighted Dad with our pas de deux.

While I sat on Dad's lap drinking my mug of hot chocolate, he read *Sand Cake.* Isabella lay quietly at his feet listening to the tale. "One summer day the bear family went to the beach, where they swam and sunned themselves on a blanket." I recited the story by heart as Dad read, and the thought of becoming a ballerina went right out of my head.

But the seed had definitely begun to take root. **I was going to be a ballerina someday,** and the name Dancing Feet stayed with me until I was a teen.

Stories and Music and Dreams Are Best Friends

"**I**t is seven o'clock. It is time for bed," Father said and kissed Frances good night." In my earliest memory I'm in my crib, and Dad is reading me *Bedtime for Frances.*

"Daddy, Daddy, there's a giant gorilla in my room."

"Sarah, that's only the shadow of the monkey Aunt May gave you for Christmas."

"Daddy, Daddy, there's a giant tiger on the ceiling."

"Sarah, that's only the shadow of your little Snuggy bear." Then Dad gave me a hug to banish all my fears.

Stories nourished my imagination and encouraged my dream of becoming a ballerina. As a toddler Mom took me to Bedtime Stories at the library. Miss Barbara always picked the best stories ever. Sitting on the floor in my pjs with Snuggy bear in my arms, I liked all the stories she read.

I can still hear Miss Barbara's gentle voice as she waved goodbye, "Sail away sweet ones on silver moonbeams as the Goodnight Parade marches into your dreams." Mom said I fell right to sleep when I got home. I remember my dreams then were always about ballerinas sailing on silver moonbeams and dancing in good night parades.

For a long time after Mom read me the story of the caterpillar who turned into a beautiful butterfly, I would wake up each morning and run to the large mirror in the hall hoping that I had turned into a ballerina.

I loved the story of the little blue engine who tried very hard and finally could do what he "thought he could," and my favorite Aesop fable was the tale of the race between the tortoise and the hare. The arrogant rabbit is so sure of himself he takes a nap, and the turtle at a slow and steady pace wins the race. These stories made me more determined than ever. I knew if I tried hard enough, I could do anything, even become the ballerina in my dreams.

Aunt May knew I wanted to be a ballerina, and she always encouraged my dancing feet. When I greeted her at the door with a turn and a curtsy, she'd say, "Sarah, you were born to dance." Every birthday and Christmas she gave me a book that brought me into the enchanting world of ballet.

In *Tallulah's Tutu,* a little girl fills her day with thoughts about ballet. Like Tallulah, all my thoughts whirled round in the enchanting world of ballet. The patio chair became my barre to practice my pliés. My little pug and I danced a pas de deux, and I called her jumps, jetés. Isabella loved the sound of the French words, too.

I delighted in all the *Angelina Ballerina* stories that Aunt May gave me. The pretty little mouse wanted to be a ballerina more than anything in the world. As she danced her way to happiness, she leaped and twirled around the house and through the halls in school, just as I did, and pirouettes were a problem for her, too.

"Be careful, Sarah. You're going to fall on Isabella," Mom often warned.

Tallulah loved fluffy pink dresses that looked like tutus. One Halloween Mom made me a pink tutu, and I wrapped the leftover tulle around my little pug. We looked grand, and Isabella Ballerina in her frou frou won everyone's heart that day.

One Christmas Eve as the littlest ballerina and I waited for Christmas morning to arrive, I read Isabella the story of *Ella Bella Ballerina and the Nutcracker.* That night I drifted into sleep to the rhythm of her snores, and Isabella Ballerina and I danced all night.

In an enchanted forest
Filled with tall fir trees glowing in the moonlight,
A little girl dances as if carried by the wind.

With the moon shining silver on her fawn coat of fur,
A little pug jetés by her side.

In the silvery light
The puppy and the ballerina create
A Glorious pas de deux

I loved going to sleep and dreaming. At the first light. I tucked the dream in my imagination, hoping to keep it safe all day so it would return again that night.

For as long as I can remember the ballerina had a permanent home in my imagination, and music gave wings to the dream. In an early memory I see Dad in the shadow winding up my music box. The ballerina on top twirls round and round to the gentle strains of the "Dance of the Sugar Plum Fairy." As I drift off to sleep, I return to that enchanting place where my dreams lived.

In a winter wonderland
Of tall oak tree heavy with snow,
A little ballerina twirls round and round,

The sparkle in her eyes

Lighting the cloudless night sky.

One morning, dawn and mist still mingling, I started banging out an unrecognizable tune on the old walnut spinet Mom played when she was a girl. In my head I was playing the "Dance of the Sugar Plum Fairy."

"Don't you think we should give Sarah piano lessons, Alice?" I heard Dad say on his way out to work.

I was just finishing my bowl of cheerios when Mom put her hand on my shoulder, "Sarah, Daddy and I think you're old enough to learn to play the piano."

When Mom and I knocked on Miss Bennet's door the next day, a thunderous outburst sent a silver-gray cat scurrying down the hall. I hid behind Mom, the top of my head barely reaching her waist. I was only six years old. At ten years old I was taller than Mom and my legs were long and lean like Aunt May's.

Miss Bennet opened the door, and a big, black fluffy dog with white patches poked his head between her legs and licked my hand. "Patches is a very gentle dog, Sarah. Don't be afraid."

When I sat at the shiny black Kawai, I wrapped my arms around the Newfoudland and gave him a hug before I began to play. The Newfoundland sat quietly with his paw on my lap.

I loved the feel of his long, silky coat. He reminded me of Nana, the beloved guardian to the children in *Peter Pan.* "Daddy, tell me about the imaginary, faraway land where Peter Pan and Tinkerbell and the Lost Boys live."

As my lessons progressed, the gentle giant felt comfortable to join in the fun, his barks keeping time like a real-live metronome. While I played "Dance of the Sugar Plum Fairy," Patches circled the room, barking in harmony to the beautiful music that I loved so much.

I loved Patches, and I loved learning to play the piano at Miss Bennet's. "Mom, when do we go to Miss Bennet's again?"

"You know, Sarah, I don't ever remember being that interested in piano lessons when I was your age, but there was no big black and white fluffy dog to welcome me then. Patches is a real charmer, almost as lovable as our Miss Isabella."

Mom understood me so well. Although I looked forward to going to Miss Bennet's, I didn't practice very much at home. Patches really was the big attraction, but I never tired of playing the "Dance of the Sugar Plum Fairy" to accompany the ballerina that was always dancing in my head.

When Mom asked after the dinner dishes were cleared from the table, "What would you like to play tonight, Sarah?" I always said "Dance of the Sugar Plum Fairy." Through the summer and even as the leaves turned golden and the evenings crisp, I played "Dance of the Sugar Plum Fairy" to prepare for the Christmas concert. At Thanksgiving I played the piece for Aunt May.

"Sarah, would you like to play the piano for Aunt May?"

"Sure, Mom."

I sat down at the old walnut spinet, the sweet aroma of Mom's pumpkin pie wafting through the air. "What would you like me to play, Aunt May?" I always asked, even though I knew what my aunt would say.

"I'd love to hear the 'Dance of the Sugar Plum Fairy,' Sarah." Sometimes the sadness buried deep inside Aunt May rose up without warning. When I played the "Dance of the Sugar Plum Fairy," a tear rolled down my aunt's cheek.

I remember it was warm that Thanksgiving, not at all like the end of November. After dinner Aunt May and I sat out on the patio listening to the *Nutcracker,* and I asked her why she had cried.

"Sarah, when I was twelve years old, I danced the role of the Sugar Plum in a Christmas recital, and the memory of performing a pas de deux with my handsome prince always makes me sad."

I just held my aunt's hand tightly, but she didn't explain why the memory made her sad until I was old enough to understand.

As the Christmas holiday drew near, the nutcracker cavalier Aunt May gave me stood tall on top of the piano. Like the prince guarding Clara in Ella Bella's dream, I felt safe with the cavalier standing watch.

"Sarah, why don't you play the Christmas carols Miss Bennet gave you?"

"I need to practice for the Christmas concert, Mom." My excuse to play "Dance of the Sugar Plum Fairy" again.

"Sarah, would you play "O Christmas Tree" for me tonight?" I could hardly refuse Dad's request three days before Christmas.

For the rest of the holiday season, I played "O Christmas Tree" and "Santa Claus is Comin to Town" just for Dad. Dad always sang along. Sitting in the green velvet chair by the piano with Isabella on his lap, her big brown eyes open wide, his robust voice, a little off key, made the ornaments on the Christmas tree shake.

But I didn't abandon the Sugar Plum Fairy dancing in my head. And the cavalier Aunt May gave me always had his special place on the piano that year.

Even on the night before my piano concert, my ballerina dream was never far away. The wind chime echoed across the lawn and the Sugar Plum Fairy danced in my head to the delicate ringing of bells. I held Isabella up by her front paws, and we twirled around until I was giddy and flopped down on the bed. But Miss Isabella's dancing paws refused to be still. Looking straight into my eyes, she made her wishes quite clear in a burst of short, high barks, "More, Sarah. More."

I picked her up, and we twirled around again. "Now we have to go to sleep, Isabella Ballerina. My piano concert's tomorrow." The wind chime stopped, and I fell asleep with Isabella cradled in my arms and dreamed the same dream I had when the snow fell quietly, and one star illuminated the sky.

> *Beneath trees with snow-rimmed limbs*
> *Glistening in the light of the moon,*
> *A little ballerina dances like the wind.*

In the morning I woke to the welcoming melody of a cardinal on a snow-rimmed branch of the kwanzan tree. I imagined the song bird singing the "Dance of the Sugar Plum Fairy."

I put on the red velvet dress Aunt May gave me for my birthday and stood before the large mirror in the hall. Raising my arms in the air, I pointed my toe and twirled into the kitchen.

"Sarah, you look so pretty. Let me fix your hair before we have breakfast."

Mom brushed my long brown hair and placed a big red

bow on top of my head that streamed down to the lace trim at my hem. Standing before the mirror in the hall, I turned round and round. Isabella stood up on her hind legs ready to be my prince. I held her up by her front paws, and before I sat down to eat breakfast, we twirled round the kitchen table. My imagination always found the place where my ballerina dream lived.

"The chocolate chip pancakes are delicious, Mom."

When we arrived at the library, the room was filled with family and friends. Patches lay quietly in a corner. I went over and sat beside my pal.

"Now Sarah Baker, our youngest student, will play Tchaikovsky's 'Dance of the Sugar Plum Fairy.'"

When I heard my name, I wrapped my arms around my gentle friend and whispered, "Wish me luck, Buddy." Patches gave a low bark of encouragement.

As I passed Dad, he handed me my nutcracker cavalier. "Remember what Aunt May told you, Sarah. In the German tradition the toy soldier's a symbol of good luck to scare the bad spirits away."

I placed the cavalier on top of the grand piano and curtsied. The stiffness in my shiny new patent leather Mary Janes reminding me that the day was special. I took a deep breath and sat down carefully, tossing out the ribbons streaming from my hair. In that moment I was in a great concert hall. As my fingers raced across the keyboard, my cavalier standing tall on the grand piano danced with the Sugar Plum Fairy in my head.

In the silence after the applause, my imagination still filled with the ballerina and my noble cavalier, Aunt May ran over and gave me a hug. "Sarah, I have a surprise for you."

"What is it, Aunt May? What is it?" My aunt's gifts were always so special. Each year on my birthday she gave me a CD of Tchaikovsky's music. Mr. T, that's what I called him then, played an important role in keeping my ballerina dream alive.

"At the ice cream parlor, Sarah."

We all went to Henry's Confectionery Shoppe to celebrate. I finished my chocolate sundae quickly and ran over and kissed my aunt. "Can I have my surprise now, Aunt May?"

"You played beautifully today, my love. Something special for my girl with magic fingers and dancing feet."

Even the package wrapped in shiny red paper with ballerinas dancing between and around silvery-white snowflakes was special. I removed the paper carefully to save in my memory box.

"Oh, Aunt May, this is wonderful," I exclaimed. On the cover of a slim book, a nutcracker cavalier with a wide mouth was smiling at me. He had on a blue and red uniform with gold epaulets on each shoulder and a silver-hilted sword by his side. "He looks just like the cavalier you gave me, Aunt May!"

"And the arrangement of the piano pieces is perfect for your level, Sarah."

Beneath a row of dancing flowers with angel's wings, large shiny ornaments of dancers from around world circled the nutcracker cavalier. A Russian in bright red with a tall furry hat kicked his booted foot high. A lady from Arabia danced with a mysterious veil across her face. And a dancer from China with a long black beard leaped into the air. As I leafed through the book, dancing figures from the ballet on every page, I could hardly keep my dancing feet still.

"Oh, Aunt May, I'm going to practice every day. I promise. Someday I'm going to play every piece for you."

But I didn't. In the spring concert I played "The Waltz of the Flowers." As my ballerina dream grew strong, I began to lose interest in the piano.

"Sarah, please practice the piano now."

"Not now, Mom. I'm listening to the *Nutcracker.*"

Creating My Own Ballet

One warm summer evening, the night sky almost too small to hold the stars smiling down on us, Aunt May and I sat out on the patio listening to *The Nutcracker* and *Sleeping Beauty*. The moonlight embraced us in its glow, and a nightingale sang a beautiful song in the shadow of the leaves shining silvery-white on the kwanzan tree. I reached for my aunt's hand. "Aunt May, why did you give up ballet?"

Her face turned somber quickly, and she spoke slowly to hold back her tears. "Sarah, I was just your age when I began to study ballet. Lessons, recitals, I loved it all. At sixteen, dancing had become the center of my life, and Grandma and Grandpa were concerned.

'May, did you finish your history report?' Grandma felt that spending so much time at the dance studio was affecting my school work.

'You look tired, May. Why don't you stay home from your lesson today?' Grandpa had been saying that often. I became suspicious when I heard them whispering in the kitchen after I went to bed. The word ballet came up frequently in the conversation.

Then there was that rainy Friday afternoon in April. I had just arrived home from school. When I entered the kitchen, a rush of wind swept past the window and the clouds grew dense and dark, a frightening forecast of what was to come. 'No homework this weekend, Mom, but I have a paper due next week. Maybe I'll stop by the library after dance class and pick up some books.'

Sarah, Grandpa walked over and put his arm around my shoulder, his face growing as grim as the storm clouds darkening the sky." My aunt paused, waiting for the pain to be far enough away to remember without tears. Then she sighed deeply.

"Sarah, I could feel Grandpa's pain as he spoke. 'May, since you'll be going to college soon, your mother and I feel dancing consumes too much of your time. The world of dance is very competitive, and it's a difficult career to pursue. We think it best that you give up ballet. You're a talented, creative young lady, and there are so many things you can do if you open your heart to them.'

I know Grandma and Grandpa thought they were doing the right thing. They only wanted what was best for me, but in that moment my whole world went silent."

Tears streamed down my aunt's cheeks, then the sobs. I put my hand on her face to stop the tears. I wanted to send each teardrop to a place where the sun always shines, and there are no storm clouds darkening the sky. I hugged my aunt for a long time and whispered over and over, "I love you, Aunt May. I love you so much."

Then my aunt placed her hands on my shoulders, tears staining her cheeks. "Now encouraging your dream of becoming a ballerina makes me happy, Sarah dear."

I heard my heart crying. I wanted more than anything to soothe my aunt's pain. We went to my room, and I took out my memory box. I read her the poem she sent on my fifth birthday.

For Sarah on her Fifth Birthday
In an emerald green meadow bordered by tall oaks
I look for my little ballerina everywhere . . .
Behind the large purple bloom
Glowing in the sunlight on the hibiscus tree,
Near the golden blossoms on the butterfly bush
Where speckled monarchs flutter their wings.

In the dappled shade under the kwanzan tree,
I see her spinning
Like a sylph with angel's wings.

"Aunt May, in my dreams I'm always spinning like an angel with wings. I know I'm going to be a ballerina someday. Maybe even a prima ballerina, Aunt May."

A shaft of moonlight entered my room. My aunt smiled and held me close. She knew her dream had become my dream now.

On rainy days, I often read the poem, and I see my aunt smiling and the large purple bloom glowing in the sunlight on the hibiscus tree and the monarchs fluttering their wings near the golden blossoms on the butterfly bush. Then the grey skies take flight, and the sun shines bright.

Then one night the moon shining bright, the roses glowing, I lay in bed waiting for sleep to arrive. The only sound the hoo-hoo-hooooo of a great horned owl. With the *Nutcracker Ballet* always a vivid memory, I imagined the roses unfurling in a glorious waltz and a dewdrop dancing around each bloom. I closed my eyes and a dream filled my sleep.

In a circle of roses
A ballerina rises en pointe.
Radiant in the silvery-blue light of the moon,

She sprinkles each blossom
With a tiny bead of dew.

Waking up at dawn, I wanted more than anything to make my dream and my aunt's dream come true. The ballerina had lived too long in my imagination. I decided to create my own ballet.

School had just ended. With the whole summer waiting, Barbara, Terry, and Patty came over in the afternoon to talk about things we could do.

"I have a great idea. Let's put on a ballet and invite our family and friends and even our pets."

"Sounds good, Sarah. I'll tell Mom to bring Ariel. What will the ballet be about?"

"It will be a dance of flowers, Barb?" The ballerinas, a perfect bouquet of pink blossoms, unfurling in a glorious waltz in the *Nutcracker* were always dancing in my head,

"Sarah, I don't like performing in front of people. Besides I've never danced before.

"I'll be the choreographer, Terry, and I'll teach you some of the steps Aunt May taught me."

"What's a choreographer?"

"The choreographer's the one who creates the steps for the ballet. It'll be fun."

"OK, I guess, but I think Teddy's too frisky to bring."

Patty loved the idea. "I know Shane will enjoy seeing the ballet with Isabella. He loves being with his friend."

For the rest of the afternoon we discussed which flower we wanted to be. When the sun began its journey behind the horizon, and ribbons of orange, vivid violet, yellow, and pale pink filled the sky, we picked a color for our flower.

Barbara wanted to be marigold as orange as her little league softball team's uniform. Softball was her thing that summer.

Patty said she wanted to be a violet blossom like the lotus rising up at dawn each morning in the small pond in her garden. Purple was her favorite color. I remember she always wore purple bows in her hair no matter what she was wearing.

As the sun lingered before the moon took charge, Terry's long blonde hair glowed. "Terry, you look like a beautiful golden-yellow daisy." Terry nodded "OK."

Of course, I wanted to be a pink rose like the Sugar Plum Fairy in her pink tutu speckled with glimmering jewels in the *Nutcracker.* My imagination was always filled with the Christmas Aunt's May's gift brought me to the place where my dreams lived.

"It's time to go home girls" Mom called from the window.

"See you tomorrow. We have lots of work to do."

Some dreams have a special place in your heart, warm as a summer breeze, green as spring, and soft as new fallen snow. That night, I had my favorite dream.

In a circle of sunlight
Slanting through the leaves of a slender birch,
A ballerina pirouettes.

In the morning I woke up as the sky grew light and was unwavering in my determination to make my ballerina dream come true.

The temperature soared in the 90s that July, and in sun or under clouds, we gathered on my patio around 8 AM to begin our warm up. We each had our own special patio chair which became our barre. "Plié down, one two three. Up, one two three."

The days, often lasting until the fireflies left trails of light, were filled with the satisfaction that comes from working hard and accomplishing my goal. At the end of each day, I was so tired I could barely crawl into bed. Isabella would curl up beside me. As the weeks went by, her big brown eyes glowing in the light of a summer moon expressed longing. I know she would have loved to be in the ballet.

The last Saturday in August, a crispness in the air promising the arrival of fall, Aunt May stopped by and gave us the confidence we needed to continue to work hard. That day we performed the whole ballet for her.

"Girls, I love the way you pas de bourrée across the patio, and you also have a lot of control when you turn. Even one pirouette is difficult to do."

When my aunt referred to our steps in ballet terms, I was more than ever determined to fulfill my dream. **Yes, I was going to be a ballerina someday!**

As we put our arms forward and lifted one leg into the air, I heard Aunt May say to Mom, "Even though they haven't had lessons, they dance like little sugar plum fairies, Alice. Sarah must be working them hard." Then turning to us, she said the magic words," Girls, you dance like ballerinas."

Aunt May left us with so many good thoughts that day. "Terrific job, ballerinas. Your ballet's going to be a great success."

The next day she brought over a stack of programs she had printed up for us.

The Dance of the Flowers

Music by Tchaikovsky (from the Nutcracker Suite)

Choreography by Sarah Baker

Costumes and Scenery

Sarah Baker, Patty Davis, Barbara
Baines, Terry Werner

Lighting by Daylight

Cast

Lotus Blossom

Patty Davis

***

Marigold

Barbara Baines

***

Daisy

Terry Werner

***

Rose

Sarah Baker

I saved the program in my memory box. I never wanted to forget the summer I first became the ballerina in my dreams.

The Day of the Performance

Each season has its beauty – a new fallen snow at sunrise, Dad's pink peonies glowing in the sun, and the spicy scent of Mom's cinnamon-red carnations. On the day of the performance nature didn't disappoint me. That morning at dawn, I stood at the window watching the gold and crimson leaves drifting down to lie on the burnt-orange grass. A squirrel scurried across the lawn, his cheeks puffed up with acorns, and a chorus of sparrows trilled their song in the kwanzan tree. One bright star shone in the sky. I made a wish. "Star light, star bright, please shine on the ballerinas today."

I quivered with the thought of the day ahead. My hands shook as I slipped very quietly into my tutu. I didn't want to wake up Isabella. The pink ballet slippers Aunt May had given me were a little small, but I still felt like Cinderella putting on her glass slipper.

As the sun grew stronger, a bright orange and black monarch taking in the warmth fluttered its wings around the lilac bush, and a goldfinch on a branch of the birch serenaded the new day. Its yellow feathers shining golden in the sunlight. He seemed to be singing "The Waltz of the Flowers." My heart rose.

I tip-toed to the large mirror in the hall. As I pointed my toe, I saw Isabella's little monkey face in the corner of the mirror. "Good morning, Miss Isabella. Come on, let's go out on the patio." There were no clouds in the sky, not the slightest threat of rain as the weather forecast had predicted. Even so late in the season the fragrant scent of roses filled the air.

My friends arrived promptly at 8 AM. Standing at the door with their arms held high and their feet turned out, the first step Aunt May taught me when I was just a toddler, they looked awesome, my favorite word that summer. Barbara's bright orange tutu complemented the tan she had gotten playing catch with her dad before arriving for practice each morning, and Patty in the palest of lavender looked like a lotus blossom rising to salute the sun. I gave an enthusiastic thumbs up. "You guys look AWESOME."

Patty proudly pointed her toe. "Grandma wrapped purple velvet ribbon around my ankles to look as if I have on toe shoes."

"That's a super idea."

Terry arrived around 9. I remember it was the only day she was late. Her face paralyzed with fear, she just stood sullenly at the edge of the patio fussing with her hair. Her hands were shaking.

"Daisy, Daisy, you look so pretty."

"Thanks, Sarah.' She tried to push away her gloom. "Do you like the ribbons Mom put in my hair?" When she turned her head quickly, an explosion of long blonde hair entwined with her bright yellow ribbons.

"You look awesome, Daisy. I wish I had blonde hair. Come on, help us put the flowers around the patio."

One Christmas Mom and I made red crepe paper poinsettias to put on our tree. They looked great and were so easy to make. With every detail of the "Waltz of the Flowers" still a vivid memory -- *pink roses unfurling in a glorious waltz, and a dewdrop dancing around each bloom* -- I taught my friends how to make paper flowers to decorate the patio. I can still see Isabella pressing her little nose to each colorful paper bloom we had arranged carefully around our "stage." Silly Iz.

With the last flower in place, Terry looked around and smiled. Patty slumped down on a folding chair. Her sighs like the hum of a bumble bee. A small pink-velvety-eared rabbit hadn't moved all morning from a spot on the lawn where the birch overhangs the grass. "I had a bunny with floppy pink velvety ears. He was so cute." The little critter finally put a smile on Patty's face.

Mom came out and shook our hands. "Great job, girls. I'm so proud of you." I hugged Mom and hoped the ballet would make her understand how much I really want to be a ballerina.

Patty's sister, the first to arrive, ran across the lawn with Shane pulling ahead, his tail wagging wildly. "Hi, Pat. You look lovely. When I called out, 'Mom, I'm going to Patty's ballet now, Shane started whining. Mom said I should take him with me. She'll be along soon."

The Labrador leaped up and lapped his long tongue across Patty's face, smearing her lightly rouged cheeks Mom had helped her put on. Wrapping her arms around her big dog, she gave him a hug. "Thanks, Buddy."

Isabella lay in a patch of shade at the back of the lawn. When Shane saw her, he dashed over and touched his nose to the tip of her nose.

I remember another day, the geraniums glorious in the sun and the begonias thirsting for a drink. Shane arrived eager to meet his new friend, and Isabella no bigger than Dad's hand. That day the big dog walked cautiously over to my chocolate monkey face pup and pressed his big nose gently to Isabella's little nose. Friends forever were sealed with that kiss.

Isabella and Shane lay side by side, their fawn and black coats shining in the sun. Terry looked longingly over to them. "Mom isn't going to bring Teddy because I'm too nervous. He can be pretty frisky sometimes."

The sun climbed higher in the sky and beamed down on the backs of my little pug and the Labrador. When they moved into the shade under the kwanzan tree, the rabbit yawned and stretched. Giving his floppy-pink ears a good shake, he hopped right up to sit next to the gentle canines.

The chatter of family and friends charged the air. Aunt May came over and gave us each a hug. "You're going to do a great job, ballerinas."

The mums lifted their golden heads to the sun, and the roses waited, fully in blossom on every branch. When the chairs were filled, Mom announced "The Dance of the Flowers will now begin." At the opening note of the *Nutcracker's* "Waltz of the Flowers," my heart began racing.

I stood at the edge of the patio, waiting, breathing deeply. When Terry made one leap into Barbara's arms, her long blonde hair entwining with the yellow ribbons seemed to give her wings, and like a super catch of a line drive, Barbara caught her with no problem at all.

"Brava, Brava," Terry's mom cheered.

Barbara's dad stood up, his enthusiastic claps resounding across the lawn. Barb turned to her dad and made a quick curtsy.

As Patty tip-toed onto the patio, a glimmer of sunlight shone on the purple velvet ribbons around her ankles. Like a lotus blossom opening its petals to greet the new day, she lifted her arms gracefully to salute the sun and didn't falter on her turn. Shane gave a low bark of approval.

A monarch flew by and fluttered around a pink rose, and my dream filled my head.

> *In a garden of roses*
> *A silver butterfly flitters its wings.*
>
> *In the circle of sunlight*
> *Slanting through the leaves of the slender birch,*
> *A ballerina pirouettes.*

If I could dream it, I knew everything would be all right. Moving in and out of the circle of light filtering through the canopy of kwanzan leaves, I fluttered my arms like butterfly wings.

Rising up on my toes, I moved across the patio with one foot in front of the other. When I made my first attempt to arabesque, one arm forward and one leg back, I felt like the ballerina on my Sugar Plum glass.

"Sarah's arabesque is good, Alice. She was born to dance," I heard Aunt May say to Mom.

Two turns and I didn't fall. Isabella barked softly to cheer me on. My little pug and Aunt May were my greatest fans.

As the music rose, I leaped around the patio in what I called my grand jeté. Isabella, no longer able to restrain herself, burst into an endless stream of short, high barks.

When I took my final bow, even Shane gave his passionate approval with several deep barks, and the rabbit scurried down his hole. I imagine he was going to tell all his friends, **"Sarah's going to be a ballerina someday."**

At the end of the ballet, family and friends stood up and cheered, and that moment was worth all the hard work. **Yes, I was going to be a ballerina. I might even become a choreographer someday.**

When Aunt May walked across the patio with great ceremony and gave us each a beautiful red rose, she whispered in my ear, "Sarah, you captured the joy of dance." My heart exploded.

That day set my ballet dream on fire and was almost as special as the frosty day in December when I had leaped over snow mounds created by the wind, and Dad shouted, "Brava, Dancing Feet. Brava." **Yes, I was definitely going to be**

a ballerina.

Then like a bear, my dream hibernated until spring and another summer passed.

Writing Sends the Clouds and the Rain Away

It was that special time of year when you didn't miss the summer blossoms. Our cardinal red mums were in full bloom, and the leaves were coasting down in a glorious tapestry of color.

"Someone's special day's coming. Have you thought about what you'd like for your birthday, Sarah?"

"Mom, I'd really like to take ballet lessons."

"We'll see, Sarah. Your father and I will talk it over. But I hope you're keeping up with your writing. Dad and I love when you share the thoughts in your head. Your stories are always so good."

That night I heard Mom and Dad talking in the kitchen. "Alice, Sarah's been wanting to dance for so long. We have to give it some serious consideration."

"Tom, I always remember my father telling May that the world of ballet was very competitive and a difficult career to pursue. I think he was right, and I don't want Sarah to get hurt. You know May never really got over having to give up dancing. Maybe next year, Tom, Sarah will be old enough to choose the right thing."

I know Mom was hoping with time my dream would go away. I went to my room and tried to read *The Secret Garden*. I read one line over and over again. "I am sure there is **Magic** in everything, only we have not sense enough to get hold of it and make it do things for us." I wanted so desperately to find the magic that would convince Mom and Dad to give me ballet lessons? When I fell asleep, I dreamed the same dream I had when I was a little girl.

> *In a pine forest*
> *Filled with candied sweets and crystal snowflakes,*
> *A little ballerina sweeps into view.*
> *Beneath trees with snow rimmed limbs*
> *Glistening in the light of the moon,*
> *She dances like the wind.*

In the morning I opened my eyes slowly. I didn't want the dream to end. The stars had faded, and the pale light of dawn was beginning to turn pink. Outside my bedroom window a chorus of thrushes serenaded the last hydrangea still in bloom.

"Come on, Iz. Let's sit out on the patio." Isabella was so loving. When I held her face in my hands to give her a kiss, her big brown eyes spoke to me, "Sarah, stop dreaming the impossible dream." Although the magic didn't happen that day, with Isabella's inspiration I decided to write a story about my little pug and her friends. I often turned to writing to send away the clouds and the rain.

I called Patty. "Pat, I'm going to write a story about Isabella and her friends. Could you bring Shane over this afternoon and tell Terry to bring Teddy? I think Barb's back from her grandmother's. I'll call and tell her to bring Ariel."

While I waited for my friends to arrive, ideas kept running through in my head. Shane had to be an important part of the tale. The Labrador and Isabella were such good friends. Terry's Springer still acted like a puppy. I knew he'd liven things up. Of course, Barbara's tabby with big green eyes and a little pink nose was just too cute not to be in the story, but she was still afraid of so many things.

In the afternoon the lawn became a fairground for our furry friends. Isabella and Shane ran through the pachysandra, the big dog always mindful that his little pal was not far behind. The low slanting sun cast a shower of golden light on the evergreens, and Isabella and Shane looked like swimmers in an emerald lake.

A program from last summer's ballet survived the winter and caught Teddy's attention. With a tail that never stopped wagging, the spaniel flung the paper around the patio. Snuggled safely in Barbara's arms, Ariel never took her eyes off the spirited spaniel.

In a final pounce, little Teddy grabbed the program in his mouth and began chomping vigorously. That kept the frisky guy still for a while. Shane and Isabella were ready for some quiet time, too. They walked side by side to their favorite spot and lay in the shade under the kwanzan tree. Ariel jumped off Barbara's lap and curled up beside my little pug. She always felt safe with Isabella.

The spaniel finished chomping and started sniffing around again. When a squirrel, his cheeks puffed with nuts, scurried by, Teddy chased the intruder and crashed into the oak tree. The critter barely escaping up the oak looked down at his foe with a frightful stare.

"Teddy can be a little reckless, but he's still young. I'm sure he'll calm down soon." Terry was always apologizing for Teddy. But the spaniel was four years old, and his behavior hadn't changed since he was a pup.

I remember the blue pansies and alyssum the color of sunshine were best friends in sunny beds bordering the lawn. Like nature flourishing around me, an idea burst into bloom. "Ariel is so sweet and afraid of so many things, I think I'll write about a kitten who climbs up a tree and is too scared to get down. All her friends come to her rescue in a desperate effort to save her from falling. What do you think, Patty?"

"Sounds great!" Patty always loved my story ideas. Barbara and Terry agreed.

Although I was still waiting for the **Magic,** that night I didn't dream. I went to sleep with only the thoughts of my story tossing in my head. Writing was always a good place for me

"Tap. Tap. Tap." I woke to the ratter-tat-tat of a woodpecker on the birch at the back of the lawn. The sky was gray, and the heavy rain through the night had turned to a drizzle. Isabella opened her eyes, stretched her front legs, and lifted up her romp to meet the challenge of the new day.

"Good morning, Miss Isabella."

"Tap. Tap. Tap." The woody's tufted crown of red feathers moved back and forth on the silvery-white birch bark.

"Come and have your breakfast, Sarah."

After breakfast I grabbed the new notebook Mom had bought me. "Come on Iz, let's sit out on the patio." The white pages glaring in the sun had their own special magic that day, and I began to write my story. The birch played an important role, and even the woody had a small part.

To the Rescue

Fall arrives early and the grass has already begun to turn yellow. In the mellow light of the sun's low slanting rays, Isabella's practicing her jetés across the lawn. Last night she danced with Sarah for quite a while, and it took her a long time to fall asleep. She's pretty tired this morning. After just a few leaps she lies down on the patio under the shade of the kwanzan tree. The only sound's a woodpecker ratter-tat-tatting on the deeply ridged bark of the birch bordering the far edge of the lawn.

Suddenly she hears a pitiful "Meow, Meow" and recognizes Ariel's cry for help. The sound seems to be coming from the birch. When she dashes over to the tree, a cloud passes in front of the sun, and the little pug can't see the kitten.

"Where are you, Ariel?"

"Meow. Meow," the frightened kitten cries out.

The cloud passes, and Isabella sees the brown-patched tabby hidden under russet leaves, her four paws wrapped tightly around a thin birch limb.

"Isabellie, I climbed up and now I'm afraid. Can you help me Isabellie? Can you help me get down?"

"Of course, Ariel." Standing on her hind legs and leaning on the tree trunk, the little pug makes several attempts to climb up. Although she's in very good shape, her paws keep sliding down the smooth birch bark.

When a little rabbit with pink velvety ears and a fluffy white tail runs across the lawn, Isabella turns to ask the rabbit for help. But rabbits are afraid of cats, she wisely thinks. He'll be no help at all.

Teddy, the Springer spaniel who lives next door, hears all the fuss and slips through the loose board in the fence. All summer he has come over to chat with his friend.

"Hi, Iz, what's happening?"

"Ariel's in the tree, and she can't get down." Ariel's his friend, too, and he wants to help. Jumping up very high, he tries several times to reach the birch limb. But he can't jump up high enough.

"Meow. Meow." His reckless behavior scares the kitten.

Isabella tries to calm her frightened friend. "Everything's going to be all right, Ariel."

"Don't worry we'll get you down," Teddy joins in. "We can get a long rope and tie a basket to one end and sling the rope over the branch of the tree and pull on the rope to raise the basket, then Ariel can get into the basket and we'll lower her to the ground," the young spaniel says all in one breath.

"I don't think that'll work, Teddy. We have no basket and we have no rope, and we wouldn't be able to throw the rope high enough anyway. But thanks for the suggestion, Ted."

Little Teddy doesn't give up. "I'll run over to our garage and get a ladder. Mr. Werner has a big ladder he uses to get on the roof. We'll certainly be able to reach Ariel with the ladder," the young spaniel says, not giving very much thought to his plan.

"Don't be silly, Teddy. How could we carry a big ladder over here? Barely a year old, little Teddy is filled with many ideas, but they aren't always wise ones.

"But that gives me an idea, Teddy. There's a small stool in my garage. If we can get it to the tree, then we might be able to jump up high enough to reach Ariel."

Before she even finishes the sentence, Teddy races to the garage.

"We'll be right back, Ariel,"

"Meow. Meow."

"Don't be afraid."

When Isabella reaches the garage, Teddy's already struggling to push the stool with his head. Together they're able to get the stool to the birch, and without stopping to catch their breath, first Isabella in one of her best ballerina leaps, then Teddy, try to reach the kitten. But they can't. Teddy, a little reckless, tries over and over again. Each time leaping higher, but he only scares the kitten.

Isabella has to admit she isn't thinking very clearly at all. There must be another way to help her friend. Very early this morning she saw Shane walking down the road on his way to visit the Smiths. Maybe he can help.

When the little pug dashes over to the Smiths, Shane's lying in the backyard under the shade of the elm. The Labrador runs over. "What's up, Iz?"

"Shane, I need your help. Ariel has climbed up a tree and can't get down."

Together they dash back to the kitten. Shane runs ahead quickly. Isabella tries doing her grands jetés, but she can't keep up with Shane's long strides. When she reaches the birch, Shane is already standing up on his hind legs with his front paws on the birch limb. But Shane's bigness only scares the kitten.

"Meow. Meow. Why did you bring Shane here, Isabellie?" She's always been afraid of the big dog and the frisky spaniel.

Shane ignores the little kitten. He's used to having others frightened by his size, but he's a gentle dog with a great big heart. Even rabbits and birds are his friend. With no trouble at all, he pulls the limb closer to the ground. He's that big and that strong.

"Come on, Ariel. Come down the branch," he calls out in a deep voice. But even Shane's voice frightens the kitten.

"Meow. Meow. I can't do it, Isabellie. I can't."

Isabella stands close to big Shane "Don't be afraid. You know Shane is our friend."

Teddy shouts, "Let me help, Isabella." Standing close to Shane, he shows the kitten he's not afraid either. "Don't be scared. Shane is our friend."

When Shane stretches up even higher, he's able to reach his head over the limb.

"Come on Ariel. Come down to Shane's head," Isabella reassures the kitten. Ariel trusts Isabella. Like a skilled tightrope walker, the kitten places one paw and then the other carefully on the slim branch, but when she reaches Shane's big head, she becomes afraid again. "Meow. Meow. I can't do it Isabellie. I can't."

"Don't be afraid. Shane is our friend." Little Teddy's concerned. "Can't you see Shane's just trying to help you."

The kitten crouches and moves slowly down the slim branch like a cat stalking his prey. But when she looks into the big dog's eyes, she becomes afraid again. "Meow. Meow. I can't do it, Isabellie. I can't."

"Turn around and go backwards, Ariel."

"Shane is our friend. Don't be afraid." Teddy's so eager to help.

When the kitten turns to back down, her tail whips across the big dog's ear. Shane doesn't move. As she tries to free her front paws tangled in the Labrador's long hair, she almost falls. "Meow. Meow. I can't do it, Isabellie. I can't."

"Yes you can, Ariel. Yes you can. We'll catch you if you fall." Teddy's suggestion doesn't encourage the kitten at all.

"You can do it, Ariel." Isabella refuses to give up on her friend.

The kitten continues slowly down the steep Shane ladder. When she reaches the middle of Shane's back and sees her friends on each side, her eyes express less fear. "Meow. Meow. Am I almost there, Isabellie?" Am I almost there?"

"You're almost there. You can do it Ariel. You can do it." Isabella and little Ted call out.

As the kitten reaches the big dog's tail, Shane shouts, "Hold on, Ariel. Hold on tightly. I'm going to let go of the branch." The Labrador lets go, and the kitten flips a short distance to the ground. When she stands up, only her head reaches over the grass, and the grass isn't very high at all.

"I made it, Isabellie. I thought I could. I thought I could."

The three dogs give her a great round of cheers. "Woof! Woof! Woof!" Even big Shane's deep bark doesn't frighten Ariel now.

"Thank you so much, friends."

Bursting with pride, Teddy shouts, "I helped, too. Didn't I Isabella?" They all laugh.

Their tails wagging or curled or straight up in the air, the band of buddies walk across the lawn chatting about their great adventure.

Another story to put away in a folder in my desk drawer. It was almost as if I knew what was waiting for me. The next day I read the story to Mom and Dad.

"You're going to be a great writer someday, Sarah." Mom gave me a hug.

Dad laughed. "Terrific little story, Sarah."

The sun was at its strongest and the air was alive with amber and gold leaves when my friends and their pets arrived the next day to listen to the story. After greeting each other with a peck on the nose, Isabella and Shane romped like puppies in the pachysandra.

The last rose had bid farewell. Teddy pounced on the fallen petals and lapped them up quickly before jumping into the evergreens with his friends.

Ariel stayed curled up on Barbara's lap, never taking her big green eyes off the frisky spaniel.

"Storytime, buddies." Shane, Miss Isabella, and even lively Ted settled down in the shade under the kwanzan tree. Glancing over to Teddy lying quietly next to Shane, Ariel jumped from Barbara's lap and walked timidly over to lie next to Isabella. Even the wind stopped to listen.

"Fall arrives early and Isabella's doing what she loves most, lying on the patio watching the leaves drifting down." The four pals sat quietly to the very last line, then burst into a spirited "Woof. Woof. Woof. Meow." I'm sure they would have clapped if they could.

"I guess Teddy's settling down. Did you notice he sat quietly the whole time you were reading, Sarah? Good boy, Ted."

Ariel now knew how much her friends cared and curled up between Isabella and Shane with Teddy right by the Labrador's side. The big and the small, the lively and the tiniest stayed good friends for a very long time.

There Are Stories Everywhere

Autumn had arrived crisp and golden the year Isabella was only four months old, and we celebrated her first Halloween without my friends. Barbara and her family were at their summer home in Maine. Terry was visiting her grandmother in California, and Patty had the chicken pox.

"Come on Iz, let's go trick or treating." I remember I wrapped my little pug from her tail to her neck in the pink tulle Mom gave me. Izzie was so excited she could hardly keep all four paws on the ground.

"Be a good girl, Iz." Holding her cute monkey face in my hands, her ears drooping down like chocolate locks, I put a little tiara on her head. Isabella was Princess Aurora and I was the Sugar Plum Fairy, of course.

Wanting to hold on to the memory forever, I wrote this little tale.

Halloween with Isabella

"You look super in your frou frou, Isabella Ballerina." My little ballerina strutted to the large mirror in the hall and tilted her head approvingly.

When we stepped out the front door, a silver-blue winged butterfly hovering around a lavender mum settled on my shoulder to welcome us. Then a leaf on the maple tree beckoned it to come and hide from the leaves drifting in the wind.

In that golden month when scary pumpkins with slanted eyes and sneering grins and friendly pumpkins with great big smiles waited at doorsteps for us, Isabella wiggled her way over ruby and copper lawns. As she romped over the earthy scents, even the disturbed leaves took notice.

Princess Aurora won everyone's heart. The Warrens and the Smiths gave Isabella yummy dog biscuits in the shape of witches with tall hats. Even old Jim Jenkins, the grouch, stood outside his house with a biscuit for the littlest ballerina.

I enjoyed writing about my little pug's Halloween, and I started keeping a journal of ideas for other Isabella stories.

Isabella Ballerina

Isabella wanted to be a ballerina more than anything in the world. Whenever she could, she practiced leaping off chairs, jumping into the air, and putting one leg forward and one leg back in a serious attempt to do an arabesque. Sometimes she would hop with her friends Red Robin and Bunny Rabbit and leap gracefully across the lawn alongside Skippy the squirrel. But she couldn't twirl and her heart was set on learning to do a pirouette. Then Willow, the Japanese chin moved into the house down the road. He could spin and spin and spin.

Will Willow be able to teach Isabella to pirouette?

Naraka, the Demon in the Night

In a long ago and faraway land a little pug leaps up a steep cliff as gracefully as a ballerina. In the light of a full moon, she sees a large hairy beast greater in size than a bear or a lion. Sarah has told her of this terror in the night. "On a mountain side after dark a wild beast roams," she said. "The night demon attacks anyone who comes in his path."

The wild thing is so close the little ballerina can feel his hot breath on her back. She leaps up the steep cliff in her grandest jeté, higher than she has ever leaped before,

Will the little ballerina escape from the terror in the night?

The Wind Horse

A horse bearing a flame on his back moves across the sky with the swiftness of the wind. In the distance a little pug watches the wind horse soar over the tall oak and into the clouds. She wants to fly with the wind horse and dance in the sky. She wants to reach the sun and the moon and the stars.

Will Isabella Ballerina's wish come true?

Although it was a confusing time for me, I didn't want to just mope around. I put my ballerina dream away in that special place in my heart and began to write again.

"Sarah, what are you writing?" "Just an idea I have about Strider. You know the greyhound who runs around the park with long, graceful strides." I always carried a small notepad with me to jot down ideas for stories I might write.

The day our class visited the zoo, I asked Mrs. Blake if we could go to the seal exhibit first. I remember I was still in a stroller when Mom and Dad began taking me to the zoo right around my birthday every year. "Daddy, can we go to see the seals?" The large elephant seals were always slamming their necks against each other. Dad used to say it was like watching a championship fight.

On a broad, flat rock jutting into the center of a circular pool that day, two large black sea lions were basking in the late morning sun. Suddenly the bulls rose up. I jotted down a few details of the legendary fight, and before I went to bed that night, I wrote my elephant seal tale

The Zoo Story

Two large black sea lions bask on a rock in the late morning sun and three playful little ribbon seals frolic in the water. With no warning at all, the sea lions rise up. Barking like angry dogs, the bulls lunge toward each other, knocking their chests together.

"Ort . . .Ort. . . Ort . . . Their spine-chilling barks piercing the air.

The large seal pummels the smaller one, pounding his chest again and again. The little guy tries to hold the bully down with one flipper, but the brute thrusts his head up and buffets the kid in the chest. The kid falls back, then sidles up again.

Snorting like a boar, the brute thrusts his neck up and batters the kid's head with his chest. The little guy moves back to gather some space. Then with a rush of threatening barks, the kid lunges forward, slamming his full weight up against the bully. The brute torpedoes into the pool. When the bully slithers back on the rock, the kid propels him into the water again. The brute's tired now and gives up the fight. In the quiet the three ribbon seals join the defeated sea lion circling the pool.

Even our Friday night visitors sparked my imagination.

The Tale of Two Raccoons

Spring has arrived and the raccoons are back doing their mischief. Patty's mom and Barbara's dad have put special latches on their garbage cans. But I look forward to our Friday night visitors, pizza night at our house. I named my night raiders Jesse and James.

The sky is already beginning to light up with the colors of sunset as I gaze out the school bus. When the bus stops at the corner of Elm to let Jeff off, I see a raccoon and recognize the patch on James' left ear. Where's Jesse, I wonder. The two were inseparable.

"Margarita pizza," Mom calls as I open the front door

After dinner I throw the pizza box into the garbage and look up into the surrounding trees for the Friday night visitors. The skilled climbers usually zip down quickly to get their tasty treat. But no raiders tonight.

I go back in the house to watch "Wild America." Just as a giant grizzly pulls a chinook from the Salmon River in Alaska and flings it to her cub, I hear the familiar thud of the falling garbage can. Jesse and James are back.

I run to the kitchen window and turn on the porch light. James is alone and stands up and stares at me.

I peer into the dark edges surrounding the ring of light. No Jesse.

The night bandit lifts the lid of the pizza box, noses in and brings the discarded scraps one by one to his mouth, chomping down with quick little bites.

In the distance I hear the rustle of leaves and high-pitched squeals. Suddenly Jesse's masked face enters the light. Close behind three little balls of fur with black and white ringed tails fluffed up like feathered boas crawl out of the darkness.

At first James ignores the little furry balls and continues to chomp. Then grasping the last few bits of pizza scraps between his teeth, he moves toward the kits and drops the remaining crusts in front of them.

I smile and think, I'll have to call the new parents Jessica and James.

There were stories everywhere. I remember the day I sat at my desk watching a spider spinning its web in the corner of the window sill in Mrs. Blake's class.

"Your stories are WONDERFULL, class. Please take out your journals and begin your new story now."

That day the tiny spider on the sill sparked my imagination.

A Busy Spider

I sit at my desk looking out the window watching a spider spinning its web in the corner of the sill. Climbing quickly to the top of a silk line, the spider spins its spinneres into position, drops down from a single thread, and scrambles back up again, its eight legs busily working. In the afternoon sun a pattern, like the spokes of a wheel, gradually emerges.

Mrs. Blake takes one of the student's stories from the sill and waves it enthusiastically in the air. "A triumph for all?"

Her arm touches the rim of the web. Pausing momentarily on the quivering silk threads, the busy spinner continues to build.

The booklet falls to the floor. As Mrs. Blake bends down to pick it up, her full skirt swirls out and brushes across the web. The busy spinner continues rebuilding.

When the delicate lacework fills the corner of the sill, the happy spider scurries down the wall. I smile and thank the spider for inspiring my tale.

Whenever I felt a little sad, I wrote. That spring my notebook was easily filled. For my birthday Mom gave me a pink leather notebook with many more pages to fill. I flipped through the notebook and placed it in my desk drawer. I would begin writing tomorrow. But tomorrow came and I didn't write. I didn't write at all for the rest of that year.

Aunt May Performs Her Magic

Each evening I lay in bed listening to the *Nutcracker* or *Sleeping Beauty* or *Swan Lake*. As my longing to become a ballerina grew strong, the Sugar Plum Fairy attended by angels with halos and gold wings was always dancing in my head.

One night I fell asleep to the gentle ringing of the wind chime, eager to meet my dream.

> *In the silvery-white light of the moon*
> *A ballerina dances like an angel.*
> *Floating through the air*
> *In harmony with the gentle ringing of bells,*
> *She rises up on her toes*
> *Reaching for the moon and the stars.*

My dreams and my imagination had become very good friends. When I opened my eyes, I saw the ballerina dancing in a sunbeam streaming across my bed. She was so lovely and so graceful. I wanted more than anything in the world to be that ballerina.

I lay in bed for a long time thinking about how to find the **Magic** that was in everything. When I finally tamed my thoughts, I ran into the kitchen. I knew there was no magic in asking Mom if I could take ballet lessons, but I never stopped trying.

"Mom, can I take ballet lessons. You promised, Mom. You promised."

"Maybe next year, Sarah. Maybe next year."

At ten years old it's hard to accept maybe next year or next month or even next week. I wanted to be a ballerina NOW. That night I heard the wind chime echoing my thoughts. "It's time. It's time to become a ballerina."

"Aunt May, please come into my room. I need to talk to you alone," I whispered to my aunt at dinner the next evening.

"What is it, Sarah? You look upset."

I spoke slowly to hold back my tears. "Mom doesn't listen when I tell her I want to take ballet lessons. She keeps saying. 'We'll see, Sarah. Maybe next year.' Can you talk to her, Aunt May? Can you? You're the only one who understands."

My aunt wrapped her arms around me. "I'll do my best, Sarah, but since your mom was a little girl, I was never able to influence her. She's as stubborn as you are sometimes, sweetheart."

I was anxious all day, and the sun was just setting when Aunt May arrived. She looked happy as she greeted Dad. "How are you, Tom?" My heart began to beat fast. "What did Mom say?"

My aunt's smile quickly faded. "I'm sorry, Sarah, I wasn't able to change your mother's mind. I wrote you a letter that may explain why she's so concerned. Then not to discourage me, my aunt whispered, "But you know how your mother is. She may come around to seeing it your way soon. She just wants what's best for you."

When she handed me the letter, I could hardly breathe. I had heard it all before, and I didn't want to understand. I thought about Mom's words and started to cry, "Tom, I feel that if Sarah had to quit after starting lessons, it would even be more difficult. You see how May's shattered dream still brings her to tears."

That night I didn't read the letter. I just tossed it in my desk drawer. A week passed, and the sunset at the end of each day filled with the busyness of school and homework made me sad. Another day without ballet.

The autumn foliage had burst into color, and Isabella and I went for our walks. When she stopped to sniff a marigold or roll on the tawny leaves, I just pulled her away. I had no patience for her dallying, and nature didn't comfort me at all.

One day on returning from our walk, I passed Mom in the kitchen without saying a word.

"Sarah, where's my pansy?"

I usually picked a yellow and violet pansy to give to Mom. She was always so pleased.

"Look Sarah. Look at this tiny face. It's smiling at you." But I didn't pick a pansy that day. I had been ignoring Mom all week, and I wasn't sorry, either.

Dad tried his best to cheer me up.

"Sarah, come and have the burgers you love."

"I'm not hungry, Dad."

Isabella understood. At night she lay beside me in bed, her head on my chest, and even in the light of the harvest moon, her dark eyes had no glow.

Aunt May tried her best to cheer me up, "Sarah, let's go to Henry's and get a hot fudge sundae."

"No thanks, Aunt May."

For weeks I just moped around the house. Then my aunt arrived smiling one night and took my hand. "Sarah, let's sit out on the patio." I knew she had something special to tell me.

"The Big Apple Circus is in town, Sarah". They say it's a real extravaganza this year. I'd like to go. Do you think you and your friends would like to join me?"

All summer Patty had been telling us about the Big Top she had seen in Cape Cod. She filled my head with silly clowns and dancing horses and people on trapezes flying through the air. As often happens when you're ten years old, I tucked my ballerina dream in that special corner of my heart, and all my thoughts turned to the greatest show on earth.

"That's great, Aunt May. I'd love to see the circus. Patty is always telling us about the Big Top she saw in Cape Cod. I know she and Barbara would love to go. Terry's visiting her grandmother in California."

"I'll pick up tickets for next Saturday." She gave me a hug, and I could feel her happiness wrap around me.

Patty called every night. "I bet they'll have horses. They always have horses." Having seen the Cape Code circus, she was the expert now.

Barbara couldn't hold back her enthusiasm. "I hope they have elephants and lions and apes. Maybe even a snow leopard. Did you know that snow leopards are called mountain ghosts because they always roam alone in the rocky mountain ranges of Tibet? Their gray-white fur with dark rosette spots help hide them, and they can leap up 30 feet to hunt their prey." Barbara knew so much about animals, and I can't think of an animal she didn't love. She wanted to be a veterinarian and a professional softball player. We all had our dreams then.

"I'm sure they'll have dogs. Right, Patty? Maybe I'll teach Monkey Face some circus tricks. She's such a smart little girl."

"They always have dogs."

"Maybe you can teach Shane some tricks. We'll call them The Roly-Poly Pug and Her Daredevil Friend." Patty gave an unenthusiastic nod. Tricks weren't Shane's thing.

All week I found it difficult to fall asleep. As I lay in bed, dancing dogs and silly clowns filled my head. I remember I came home from school the day before we were to go to the circus and tied an old stovepipe hat on Isabella that I had worn one Halloween. Changing quickly into my jeans, I put on my old Orphan Annie wig, matted from years of playing pretend. "Come on Iz. Let's play dancing clowns. I cartwheeled and tumbled around my room, with Isabella leaping up in her best jetés. Then we'd flop on the bed and start all over again. We were clowns right up until it was time to go to bed. The circus had already begun to perform its magic or should I say Aunt May had performed her magic? I hadn't dreamed or thought about being a ballerina all week. We were going to the CIRCUS.

Drum Roll, Please

The sky was still dark when I woke up, my head filled with beautiful ladies doing tricks on the backs of galloping horses. When Patty and Barbara arrived, ribbons of pink and orange streamed across the sky waiting for the sun to grow strong.

"Is Aunt May here yet?"

"It's too early. She said she'd pick us up around nine. Let's sit outside and wait on the patio." Isabella dashed across the lawn and greeted us with generous lollypop kisses. She was as excited as we were. You'd think she was going to the circus.

The time passed too slowly. I remember it was like waiting for Christmas morning to arrive, and Patty continued to feed my imagination. "I know they'll have dogs. They always have dogs doing fantastic tricks."

At exactly 9 am Aunt May pulled into the driveway. When I ran up and opened the car door, Isabella jumped into the front seat.

"Not today, Monkey Face. We're going to the CIRCUS!" I can still see Isabella walking sullenly back into the house as we pulled away, her head and tail hanging low.

"I'm so sorry, Iz."

The cars on the expressway were bumper to bumper, and the tunnel had narrowed down to one lane. It felt as if we weren't moving at all. When we exited the tunnel and my eyes adjusted to the sun, cars were at a standstill at every corner. Angry horns and sirens demanding to be heard.

"Oh, Aunt May we're never going to get there in time."

"Don't worry, Sarah, we'll be there soon."

At last, a big blue tent with a ribbon of gold stars circling the words **BIG APPLE CIRCUS** appeared in the distance.

"There it is, Aunt May! There it is!"

When we got close enough to hear the music, my aunt parked in the nearest garage. The attendant counted out the change like a clock running down. I guess he had never been to the circus.

"Hurry, Aunt May. Hurry." We dodged around the crowds and ran down the street, keeping pace with the carnival tempo. At the entrance three white-faced clowns with bulbous red noses and wild tufts of flaming orange hair were spinning plates on a stick.

"The clowns look like mandrils, those old-world apes with colorful red and blue faces." Barbara always shared her knowledge of animals with us.

Several vendors standing in front of brightly painted carts were selling cotton candy and roasted nuts and frankfurters on a grill. The one in a tall red and white striped hat selling lollipops looked like the feisty cat who came to Sally's house to teach her tricks on a rainy day. I always loved *The Cat in the Hat.* "Bump! Thump! Thump! Bump!" Mom said my journey into writing began with the word BUMP. I used to scribble the word on all my books and even on the wall over my bed. Mom wasn't too happy about that.

"Have no fear! Have no Fear! My lollipops are all tasty good!" the vendor shouted, waving his pops with grimacing faces in the air.

"Would you like a lollipop, girls?"

"No thanks, Aunt May." We were too excited to eat. I just bought a small bag of rainbow circus peanuts and put them in my pocket to share with Isabella when I got home. Mom always put some in my Easter basket with chocolate bunnies and cream-filled eggs. At ten years old and not feeling quite grown up, the chewy treats in my pocket were as comforting as bringing Snuggy bear with me.

"Boy, this is going to be great!" Barbara exclaimed as we took our seats in the first row. "I hope they'll have Bengal tigers and Kodiak bears. Did you know the Bengal tiger is the national tiger of India?"

"Sorry, girls. There won't be any tigers or bears, only animals that have been humanely trained," Aunt May quickly said.

I don't think Barbara was disappointed at all. All the animal acts were absolutely sensational.

And there were clowns, of course. So many clowns. Two in billowing purple pants roamed up and down the aisles with a colorful array of balloons trailing behind. When the zaniest one reached over to shake my hand, he almost fell into my lap. "Aunt May, this is so much fun."

The year before Barbara and I had watched the *Mary Poppins* movie together, and we loved the jovial Chimney Sweep. His song still pops unannounced in my head.

Chim chiminey

Chim chim cher-ee!

The clown in shoddy pants, baggy at the knees, swishing a big broom over a spotlight on the floor wasn't jovial at all. He looked so glum.

"That's just silly." Barbara liked things to be real.

"That's the idea, Barb," and we both laughed.

Then a daredevil acrobat on a unicycle performed a body-flip with his bike between his legs. "Girls, I read that he's the first unicyclist ever to perform such a daring feat."

The cyclist flipped several more times to the roar of the crowd. In this moment my ballerina dream tucked safely in a corner of my heart, I gave my aunt a hug. "Thanks, Aunt May. Thanks so much."

In the center arena, the ringmaster in a black top hat steps into a circle of light, his red frock coat billowing behind. "Welcome to the **Greatest Show on Earth.** Drum roll, please." Trumpets blare to the beat of brass drums, and a slim young man on a fine chestnut horse canters around the ring. Sending up a cloud of dust as he bounds into a gallop, he waves to the crowd and shouts, "Let the fun begin."

Radiant in a jeweled lavender leotard with purple plumes rising high from her head, a lady with long blonde hair enters the spotlight. With a crack of her whip, six stately white steeds, purple plumes rising high from their manes, prance around the arena. As they speed up, their plumes and manes entwine and flare out.

"Aunt May, the horses look as if they're flying."

"They do, Sarah?"

Her jewels sending out laser beams of light, the lady leaps onto the lead horse. As her courtly white steed parades in a high springy step around the ring, she bounds through a gold hoop as easily as a child jumps rope. The purple plumes on her head trailing behind like a shooting star.

When I got home, I tried to teach Isabella to jump through my hula hoop. After several weeks of encouragement and lots of patience and tasty treats, Izzie jumped once or twice to show me she could. "Good girl, Iz" Then taking her leg-locked stance, she refused to do it again. Jumping through hoops just wasn't Isabella's thing, and she could be pretty stubborn sometimes.

The lady and her steeds exit to roaring cheers, then a quiet before the air recharges with excitement. Two spirited horses strut into the circle of light. Mirroring each other, they trot to the one, two, three count of a waltz. Rising to a canter and moving in unison, sideways and forwards and back, they even pirouette.

Two boys in back of us in New York Giant shirts stand up and shout, "To the right. To the left. Step up guys. You're doing great." I remember we echoed their rousing cheer on our drive home.

In their grand finale, the horses circle the arena to a heroic burst of trumpets and clarinets. As they step, step, step, their heads swaying, their manes flowing, all four hoofs in perfect harmony, they bow down on one knee. The applause is unrestrained.

"Aunt May, do you think the horses have a choreographer?"

"Almost as good as you are, sweetheart." My aunt always kept my ballerina dream alive.

Drums roll. A lady in a gold sequined leotard performs somersaults and back bends and amazing gymnastics on the back of a black Arabian trotting around the arena like a sleek racehorse.

"Do you think you could do somersaults on a horse, Dancing Feet?" Patty shouts above the roar. She never forgot the cartwheels I did when I was in kindergarten.

"No way."

Electricity charges the air. The next act really wins Barbara's heart. Four black and white Russell Terriers race around the ring behind chocolate miniature horses with long shaggy manes. Leaping up on the small horses' backs, the terriers stand on their hind legs and somersault over and over again.

"I just love Russell Terriers."

I can't think of an animal Barbara didn't love. I always remember the time she told us she saw hyenas on TV snuggled in their trainer's arms. I have to admit I'm still not convinced.

"Sarah, can you imagine Shane or Isabella doing somersaults on the back of a horse?" Patty shouts.

"Maybe not a somersault on a horse's back, but I'm definitely going to teach Isabella some tricks when I get home."

"Girls, did you read the sign when you came in? All the dogs come from The California Animal Rescue Center."

"Wow! That's terrific." Barbara cries out. "Those terriers were incredible.

Without time to take a breath, the band blares another lively tune. I remember Miss Parker in kindergarten use to play that song when we were getting ready to go to the playground after lunch. "Aunt May, what song is that?"

"Roll out the Barrel."

Then a Labrador races around the ring working his front legs rapidly over a large wooden barrel. Inside the cask a terrier spins around like a hamster on a running wheel.

"I bet Shane and Isabella could do that."

"I don't think so, Sarah." Patty is adamant. "Shane doesn't like doing tricks."

I know this wasn't the moment to discuss whether Shane could be taught tricks. But when Isabella resisted the ballet steps that I tried to teach her, Dad always said, "Patience,

Sarah. Be patient. Praise and patience and a treat or two and she'll come around."

A large black and white pig rolls out a red carpet with his big pink nose. When he walks up to the microphone and sings a squeal and an oink, Barbara exclaims, "I wish I had a pig for a pet. They're so lovable, and they're really smart."

Patty and I just shrug our shoulders. Neither of us long for the affection of a pig no matter how smart he is, but Barbara loved every animal. In high school she volunteered at the Second Chance Rescue Center. I remember Patty and I fiercely protesting when she brought home a mouse and asked us to take care of him. Ugg! She rescued two kittens, a chihuahua, and three white mice. Her mother finally drew the line. "NO IGUANA, Barbara!" Imagine, an iguana. With their scaly bodies and spiny backs, they looked like dragons to me, and the sharp nails on their claws were really scary. No iguanas for me.

"What time is it, Aunt May?" "It's almost two o'clock. The show will be over soon.

"Oh, no," we cry out.

In the staggering final acts, trapeze artists risking their lives seem to be swinging over the clouds and beyond the horizon. The aerialists remind me of the ballerina in my dream reaching for the moon and the stars, and just for a moment I allow my dream back, secretly longing to be with them in the sky.

"That's impossible. People aren't supposed to be able to do things like that. Maybe they're robots." The world of robotics really captured Barbara's imagination. She was way ahead of Patty and me and was already very interested in Artificial Intelligence. It was always clear to me that Barbara would go into some field of science. When she told us in high school that she wanted to be a veterinarian, I wasn't at all surprised.

In the last act tightrope walkers forming a seven-person pyramid defy human boundaries. A numbing silence, a gasp, then the audience stands up and cheers. They were still applauding as we left.

The drive home was so much fun.

"Did you see ____?"

"Weren't the dogs ______?"

"What about the men on the flying trapezes?"

Even Aunt May joined in our enthusiastic cheer. "To the right. To the left. Step up, guys. You're doing great."

For weeks we talked about the wonders we had seen. I didn't have to run away with a traveling circus. That year the circus had a small place in my imagination, but my ballerina dream was still Number One. Aunt May continued to keep my ballerina dream alive. The next Sunday we went to the Metropolitan

Museum of Art to see Degas's sculpture of *The Little Fourteen-Year-Old Dancer.* The delicate featured dancer posed gracefully with her head held high and her shoulders back.

"Her feet are pointed in fourth position. Aren't they, Aunt May? She's so lovely."

I stood before the ballerina for a long time, my feet in fourth position, my head high, and my shoulders back. I remember thinking maybe this would be as close as I get to becoming a ballerina. Then I was angry at myself for letting the circus take away my dream even for a moment.

Moving On

It took only one Halloween dance for Patty and Barbara to become interested in boys. That year while my friends were sipping sodas in the school cafeteria hoping to catch a guy's eye, I returned to writing, the ballerina in my dreams dancing with me every step of the way. My teacher in seventh grade recognized a talent blossoming. He was very encouraging. The day after I handed in "A Glorious Pas de Deux," Mr. Mason called me to his desk. "Sarah, you're a very good writer. May I read your dream to the class?"

"Sure, Mr. Mason." A beam of sunlight shone on the water in the fishbowl on the window sill and a beautiful rainbow appeared. As he read, I traveled over the rainbow to that special place where my dreams lived.

A Glorious Pas de Deux

When the sunset surrenders to night, a little girl lies in bed listening to the music of *Sleeping Beauty.* Drifting into sleep, she returns to the enchanting world of ballet.

The curtain rises,
And a golden globe beams a circle of light
On the center of the stage.
In the radiant ring a ballerina pirouettes,
Her golden tutu glimmering
 Like stardust on angel's wings.
As she sweeps across the stage
In harmony with the music of a harp,
A noble prince in a gold buttoned vest
Lifts her high above the trees
And the clouds and the moon.

"I loved your ballerina dream, Sarah. I wish I could write like you," Patty said on the way home on the school bus. Although the circus was wonderful, I was happy to be back where my ballerina dreams lived.

Mr. Mason published my poem in *Fun to Read,* the middle school's literary magazine, and Mom and Dad were so proud. When we returned to class after the holidays, he asked us to write a vivid description of someone we loved.

I remember sitting at my desk watching the snow cover the slide and the swings and a basketball waiting in the school playground for spring. My thoughts frolicked with the snow-flakes dancing in the wind and wandered to Miss Isabella. Soon a story began racing across the blank white page. A feeling that was and still is exciting for me.

My Little Pug

I was only four years old when my monkey face pug came to live with us. Weeks before Miss Isabella's arrival, Mom and I went to the bookstore and picked out several books about the little dogs with big brown eyes and a W of wrinkles on their foreheads.

As I lay in bed snuggled up with Snuffy bear, I listened with great expectations to the pug tales Mom read. The pictures of pugs on the cover doing funny things made me laugh.

And then the day arrived. The sun was bright, the roses in bloom, and the butterflies fluttered around the lilac bush as they waited with me for my little pug. When I heard Dad pull into the driveway, I ran out to meet him.

"Come see what I have, Sarah?"

Snuggled in Dad's lap was the tiniest puppy I had ever seen. Dad placed the puppy gently in my arms. The big red bow around her neck reminded me of the story Dad told me the night before. I had gone to my bed early so tomorrow would come quickly. Dad came in my room and sat down next to me.

"Sarah, would you like to hear the story of Pompey, the beloved pug to William, the Prince of Orange of the

Netherlands?"

"Where's the Netherlands, Daddy?"

"Let's look on your globe. The Netherlands is this small country between Belgium and Germany."

I loved when Dad and I looked at my globe. My world always grew so much bigger.

"Pompey's story is true, Sarah. The beloved pug lies at Prince William's feet on a tomb in a church in the Netherlands. Maybe we'll go to the Netherlands someday and see Pompey's sculpture at Prince William's feet.

I saved the story in a corner of my imagination for our trip to see Pompey. I can hear Dad's voice now as I remember.

"Sarah, William, Prince of Orange, had many pugs but his most cherished companion was Pompey. One night an assassin sneaked into the prince's tent. In haste the little pug leaped up on his master's head to warn him of the intruder. The prince woke up in time to stop the attack.

To honor the pug for saving his life, Prince William bestowed upon Pompey the title of Pug of the Ruling House. When Prince William came to England carrying Pompey in his arms, the little pug had an orange ribbon around his neck, a symbol of his royal position in the House of Orange."

I loved the story very much. "Daddy, I'm going to love my

little pug very, very much. Like Pompey she's going to be special." I kept my promise, too. On the Fourth of July, I always tied a red, white, and blue ribbon around Isabella's neck as a symbol of her American heritage.

Mr. Mason hung my story on the bulletin board. At the end of the school year, he said, "Save this story, Sarah. It's very good."

Thanks, Mr. Mason, you played an important role in my life.

In one of my earliest memories, I'm snuggled on Mom's lap holding little Snuffy bear while she reads *Goodnight Moon.* "And there were three little bears and a pair of kittens and a little toy house and a young mouse," -- words had already begun to perform their magic.

Every year Mom and Dad tucked a book in my Christmas stocking. My favorite Beatrix Potter books are still lined up on the shelves of an old rosewood bookcase in the corner of my room.

I remember one summer day, all the flowers in bloom and patches of clouds gliding by, I read Isabella *The Tale of Peter Rabbit.* Curled up like a basketball on my lap, her big brown eyes gleamed. As soon as I read, "His mother put him to bed and made some chamomile tea," Isabella leaped down, looked straight into my eyes, and pleaded with short, high barks.

"More, please, Sarah. More."

"No more today, Monkey Face."

Then, comforted by the sun, Isabella lay at my feet. Soon her legs moved back and forth rapidly. I imagined she had returned to that special place where her dreams lived, the home of her great, great, great grandparents.

> *On a steep cliff a golden roofed palace*
>
> *Glistens in the moonlight*
>
> *Two stone lions*
>
> *Stand guard at the palace gate.*
>
> *Like the guardian statues,*
>
> *Isabella keeps watch over her master's stately domain.*

Mom always said, "Sarah you certainly have a very vivid imagination" Stories and my little pug nourished that part of me.

Soon I was telling and writing my own tales. In nursery school even before I could write, I was telling Mrs. Monroe stories which she wrote down for me in my creative journal. I often wonder if my new dream had already begun that long ago.

In eighth grade I wrote a story influenced by Isabella and Dad's Pompey tale.

Kala, the Cherished Companion of the Empress

High on a hill a golden-roofed Palace of Love and Courage glistens in the noon sun. Under the shade of a large fig tree, Kala lies in a bed of yellow dahlias. On a high branch of the ancient banyan tree, a burnt-orange chested thrush shining golden in the sun sings a flutelike melody. The little pug rises up to dance to the beautiful song. Turning quickly, she jetés across the perfectly trimmed grass. All the pugs in the palace of the Empress could dance, but Kala was her Royal Sovereign's prima ballerina.

Respected for her dancing skills and the W of wrinkles on her forehead resembling the Chinese character for princess, Kala was her Majesty's most beloved pug.

When Kala rode in the imperial gold chariot curled up in the folds of her lady's royal robe, the maidens in the court always dressed her in a red velvet cape and placed a small gold coronet on her head.

Kala loved her Empress, and like the stone lions that stood guard at the palace door, she protected her Sovereign Ruler. One night on the eve before a great storm, Kala was curled up at the foot of her Majesty's gilded bed. In the silence she heard a creaking noise on the ancient wooden-plank floor. Peering into the darkness, she saw a large figure hovering in the corner of the royal bed chamber. Kala knew her Empress was at war with the neighboring province. She feared her Majesty was in great danger. Emboldened by her desire to protect her Sovereign, she jumped from the bed and ran as fast as a cheetah through the great hall and roared like a lioness protecting her cubs.

In domed tents at the foothills of the palace, her Majesty's loyal warriors awakened to the urgent call echoing over the hillside. Donning armor in haste, they ran up the steep hill and arrived in the royal chamber just as the assassin raised his sword over their Sovereign's head. The Empress was saved, and Kala was esteemed for her courage.

With great pomp and ceremony, the Empress bestowed upon Kala the title of Beloved Companion to the Supreme Ruler and her Royal Family. When her Majesty held court, people came from every part of the province to honor the little pug.

"Kala, Prima Ballerina, dance for my royal subjects," the Empress always said.

In that far away Palace of Love and Courage high on a hill in an ancient land, her Majesty's cherished companion danced every day for the royal court, and nestled in the folds of her Majesty's robes, she rode every day in the imperial gold chariot. And ever after pugs have been revered for their bravery and their royal lineage and their "dancing paws."

After Mrs. Clark read my story to the class, my friends came all the time to visit Miss Isabella Ballerina, and Isabella's behavior always proclaimed her royal and ancient heritage.

"Up. Up. Jeté, Isabella Ballerina." My friends cheered after each performance, and Isabella was so pleased. Yes, the limelight suited my little pug well. She and I were born to dance.

On cold, winter nights, the wind blowing strong, we would curl up by the fire, and I'd read her a story. Maybe it was another Beatrix Potter tale or a story about a ballerina. Soon she would be fast asleep, her snores drowning out my words. I didn't mind. I always imagined her returning in her dreams to the faraway land of her ancestors.

> *High on a mountain in a long ago and faraway land,*
> *Purple-blue irises circle a cherry tree flourishing in the sun.*
>
> *A little pug lies under the tree*
> *Watching a blue silver-studded butterfly*
> *Quivering around an iris in full bloom*
>
> *Shining rosy-pink in the sun,*
> *A finch alights on a branch of the cherry tree.*
> *The little pug rises and dances to the bird's sweet song.*

The Sound of Bells

Another year went by, and the ballerina still lived in my dreams. Then in a summer too hot for even the leaves to stir, my dream came true.

School had just ended. On the last day in June, Patty and I sat on a park bench under the shade of a wide-spreading maple tree planning how to fill our days with fun things to do. Terry had moved to California, and Barbara was busy playing softball and volunteering at the Second Chance Rescue Center.

"There's a swimming course starting next week at the Y, Sarah. Let's sign up for lessons. Terry took the course last year. She said they even teach you to dive."

"Sounds good, Patty."

"My family's going to the shore for two weeks in August. Maybe you can come with us.

It'll be fun."

"Thanks, Patty, but I have to take care of Isabella. Mom

will be working this summer." Taking care of Miss Iz was never a problem. Having reached the age when keeping in shape was important, I especially enjoyed our long walks together. Isabella and I even looked forward to doing yoga each morning.

As the sun grew strong, the temperature soared. "Patty, let's get a lemon ice." In the storefront window next to Henry's Confectionery Shoppe, a new sign, **Miss Peggy Hanson's Dance Studio,** got my immediate attention. "Let's check it out, Pat."

The brass pointe slippers on the newly painted red door sent my heart racing. "It's a ballet studio!" In that moment of chance, that serendipitous moment, I saw myself on pointe in a sparkling pink tutu.

"Hurry, Patty. Hurry." Flinging the door open, I dashed two steps at a time up a very long flight of stairs. In a large mirrored room at the top of the staircase, a ballet class was just ending. Two young dancers, their faces glistening with beads of perspiration, walked by carrying tote bags.

"I still can't do a pirouette," the girl with long, blonde hair said, her hands tucked sulkily into the pockets of her jeans. "Lorna, let's go home and practice."

"That's a good idea, Betsy. Miss H said I have to work on my port de bras. When I saw my reflection in the mirror, my arms seemed to be flagging down a plane." Even the freckles on the dancer's face couldn't hide her disappointment, and it didn't surprise me at all that the musty smell of hard work still lingered in the air.

A young woman wearing black tights and a black leotard came out of her office to greet us, "I'm Miss Hanson. Are you here to enroll in a ballet class?"

With no hesitation at all I answered, "Yes." Not for a moment did I consider what Mom would say. My only thought was **I'm going to be a ballerina.** Maybe even a **"prima"** ballerina someday.

"I can't. I'll be away this summer," Patty answered just as quickly.

On the way home I hardly said a word, my head filled with ballerinas dancing to the sound of bells. "See you later, Pat."

When I ran into the kitchen, Mom was preparing dinner. "I just signed up to take ballet lessons, Mom." Mom continued mashing the potatoes. "Did you hear me, Mom?"

After a long pause and in a voice that expressed no enthusiasm at all, Mom turned and said, "OK, Sarah, but promise you'll keep up with your reading and writing this summer."

Mom didn't object. That was all I heard. Giving her a quick hug, I raced into my room to look for my black tights.

"I picked up *Little Women*," she called after me. "The librarian said *The Call of the Wild* would be back in a couple of days."

I blocked out what Mom was saying. I didn't want the joy I was feeling to end. At dinner Dad was smiling. "I hear you signed up for ballet lessons, Dancing Feet."

"Dad, I think Miss Hanson's so nice. She's pretty, too. She had on a black leotard and tights, Mom. Even the girls walking out at the end of class had on black leotards. Do you think I can get a leotard and maybe a tote bag for my ballet slippers?"

"We'll see, Sarah. We'll see. Maybe you can save up and buy them with your allowance?" I know Mom was hoping this would just be a summer fling.

When Aunt May couldn't convince Mom to give me ballet lessons and she saw how upset I was, she had written me a letter which I had never bothered to read. After dinner I went to my room and got the letter tucked in an old notebook in my desk. I read it twice.

"Sarah, dear, your mother may be right. Dancing becomes a ballerina's whole life. When I was studying ballet, I took lessons three times a week after school. In winter when dusk arrived early, I walked home very tired with the streetlamps lighting my way and then had to do my homework. On Saturdays I arrived at the studio promptly at 9 a.m. After a strenuous two-hour class and a yogurt snack, I was off to pilates and maybe a run, returning to the studio in late afternoon to practice again. Some days I stayed to work on my pirouettes until bands of red and orange streamed across the sky, and the moon often lighted my way home. Would you be willing to work that hard, Sarah?"

The letter didn't discourage me at all. I never thought it would be easy, but my dream of becoming a ballerina was more real and closer than it had ever been.

I put the letter back into the drawer and tried reading *To Kill a Mockingbird,* but I couldn't even get through the first paragraph. Reaching for a Snicker bar on the night table, I pulled my hand back quickly. The tall, blonde ballerina was so slim.

Remembering that frosty day in December so long ago when my dream of becoming a ballerina was only a dream, I put on the *Nutcracker* to calm the thoughts running through my head. On the opening note Isabella ran to me, and we waltzed around the bed. It didn't matter at all that our pas de deux wasn't ready for the City Ballet. **I was going to be a ballerina.**

"Sarah, try to go to sleep now. You said your lesson was at ten tomorrow."

"OK, Mom." Isabella snuggled her head next to my pillow. Her snoring resounded through the room, but only the music of the "Waltz of the Flowers" and all the wonderful thoughts running through my head kept me awake that night – "I was going to be a **"prima"** ballerina someday."

When I finally fell asleep, I dreamed the same dream I had on the eve of Christmas when I was seven years old.

> *In an enchanted forest silver in the moonlight*
> *And the sound of bells ringing everywhere,*
> *The Sugar Plum Fairy pirouettes lighter than air*
> *In the arms of her handsome cavalier.*

Even today I still return to that place where my ballet dreams live. When I am sad, they brighten my day.

In the soft gray mist of early morning, a bright orange-winged monarch fluttered its wings around a lavender bloom on the butterfly bush. The sun was just beginning to dust the grass gold, and daylilies sweetened the air. A beautiful beginning to a day that held so much promise, and the memory lives on as I write.

It was Wednesday, just an ordinary Wednesday. I woke up and my dream was still vivid.

> *The Sugar Plum Fairy pirouettes lighter than air*
> *In the arms of her handsome cavalier.*

Like our morning glories opening their petals to greet the new day, Isabella opened her eyes at the first light. Stretching her front legs across my chest, she lifted up her rump. "Super puppy dog, Miss Iz."

Accompanied by sparrows trilling their song in the lilac shrubs outside my window, I rose up to salute the sun. Sitting alert in the corner of my room, Isabella waited.

"Chair pose, Iz." Izzie dashed over and sat up on her hind legs. She had easily mastered this pose, and you could see by the twinkle in her eyes she was pleased.

As thoughts of the challenge of the day ran through my mind, my heart began racing. To hush my heart, I sat on the floor in my meditation pose. Isabella quickly curled into my folded legs. We stayed in this pose until I quieted my speeding heart. I hoped the calm would remain with me all day.

In our final pose, Miss Iz lay across my stomach and lapped a gentle kiss across my cheek. "We're supposed to be still, silly girl." But Isabella knew what I needed that day. She understood me so well.

I remember Patty called right after breakfast. "Sorry, Patty. Not this morning. Then my voice rose with excitement. "I have a DANCE class. Call you when I get back."

"Bye, mom. The DANCE class should be over about noon."

With a rainbow of color shining on her through the stained-glass front door, Isabella waited to wish me good luck. When she leaped up and lapped her tongue across my cheek, I held her monkey face in my hand and kissed her wrinkled brow, "Thanks, little girl. I'll tell you all about it when I get back."

Even as the sun grew strong, I ran down the treeless streets into town to the dance studio. Thrusting open the red door, I bolted two by two up the long flight of stairs. At the top step my legs suddenly refused to go any further. As long as I could remember, I wanted to be a ballerina. Now that the moment had arrived, I couldn't keep my heart still.

I stopped to take a deep breath and noticed a painting entitled *Ballet at the Paris Opera* on the wall outside the studio. I recognized the artist's name. "Sarah, we'll have to come again to see Degas's lovely paintings of ballet dancers," Aunt May had said as we admired his sculpture of the fourteen-year-old ballerina that Sunday afternoon at the museum.

In the corner of the painting the corps de ballet gathered to watch the principal dancers. The young ballerinas looked as perfect as a bouquet of long stem roses. Their diaphanous gowns flecked with pale pink rosebuds billowed over long, slender legs.

Surrounded by a forest of pastel green and yellow and blue, the central dancer on pointe raised her arms to the sky like a delicate hibiscus opening its petals at the break of dawn, and her gown glittered with tiny specks of gold. The lovely ballerina gave me the courage to walk into the studio. **I'm going to be a ballerina.**

Reflected in the large mirror covering one wall, a young dancer was warming up. She lifted her leg from the barre and walked over. "You can change in the dressing room. One of the girls will tell you which locker to use for your clothes."

I looked down at my tee shirt and tights and quickly hid my ballet slippers behind my back. I wasn't ready to enter the world I had dreamed of for so long.

The ballerina noticed my uneasiness. "You can put your shoes in one of the empty lockers."

In a room lined with benches and lockers like our school gym, the two dancers I had seen the day before were chatting. The tall, thin girl introduced herself, "I'm Betsy. This is Lorna. I think you'll love taking lessons with Miss Hanson. She's great." Immediately my heart stopped pounding. My dream of becoming a ballerina was real. I knew nothing bad could ever happen again.

As I put on my ballet slippers, I saw my aunt smiling. I was fulfilling her dream as well. The dream we shared since I was a little girl.

"Good morning, Sarah." Miss Hanson looked even prettier than I remembered. She was wearing pink tights and a pink leotard with a short skirt wrapped around her waist. Her long hair was tied up neatly in a ponytail. Today when I pull my hair back in a ponytail, I think of Miss H. So many things remind me of her. "Hold your shoulders back and your tummy in at all times, dancers," she often said. When I walk, my feet turn out in first position, just as I remember hers did.

"This is Sarah Baker, class. She'll be joining us today. Everyone to the barre, please. First position."

Placing one hand on the wooden handrail, I turned my feet out. Aunt May had taught me all the five basic feet positions when I was a little girl.

In the corner of the studio an old mahogany upright piano demanded little attention in the large mirrored room until Ellen, Miss Hanson's sister, sat down to accompany the lesson. Then the piano took charge as we synchronized our steps to the music she played. I had been dancing to Tchaikovsky's ballets since I was a little girl, and it was no problem at all for me to follow the music and Miss Hanson's rhythmic clapping.

"Plié down __ One, two, three, four.

"Up__ One, two three, four."

"Sarah, turn your right foot out and hold your back straight. That's nice, dear." When Miss Hanson placed her hand gently on my shoulder, I realized very quickly that even a simple plié required more discipline than dancing around my bedroom with Isabella in my arms.

"All to the center now. Fifth position. Tendu, please."

I looked around to see what the others were doing. As I stretched my leg out to the front, to the side, and to the back," my heart began racing, and my thoughts ran wild. Am I awake or is this a dream? Is it so long ago my dream first began?

"Sarah, hold your head up high." Miss Hanson's voice brought me back. The hands on the clock at the back of the studio were moving too quickly.

"You all have to work on your pirouettes, but everyone's port de bras has improved. Practice at home, and I'll see you on Friday. Sarah, you did very well. Did you enjoy the lesson?"

"Yes, Miss Hanson. Very much." Promising to practice at home, I walked out of the studio slowly wishing the class could have lasted forever.

"Lorna and I are stopping for a coke. Would you like to join us, Sarah?"

The coke tasted so good and so cold, cooling my dry throat. Betsy told me her first lesson brought her to tears. I knew we were going to become good friends. We chatted a while, but I was anxious to get home to tell Mom and Dad about the lesson.

"See you Friday." The thought sent shivers down my spine.

Even carrying my ballet slippers home in a brown paper bag didn't bother me now. I had taken my first step into the world I had dreamed about for so long.

Heat rose from the pavement. Ignoring the beads of perspiration running down my cheeks, I ran all the way home. Isabella was the first to greet me. "Oh, Izzie, it was great. Someday I'll ask Miss Hanson if I can bring you to class. Miss Hanson's so nice." Then holding Isabella tightly in my arms, I twirled into the kitchen.

"Mom, I just love ballet, and Miss Hanson's really nice. I stopped for a coke after class with a couple of the girls. Betsy told me she had taken lessons with two other teachers, but Miss Hanson was the 'best.' Miss Hanson even liked the way I held my arms in port da bras." In a burst of enthusiasm, the magical words, port da bras, port da bras, repeated over and over in my head.

"Look, Mom." I raised my arms in front as if carrying a big beach ball. As I moved through the basic arm movements from first to fifth position, I remembered Degas's painting and tried to reach up to the sky as gracefully as the beautiful ballerina.

"Nice, Sarah."

"When's Aunt May coming home, Mom?".

"Aunt May won't be back until the end of the week."

Waiting to tell Aunt May wasn't easy. My enthusiasm even excited Isabella. She kept following me around, jumping up and down, and dashing between my legs. You'd think she was going to be a ballerina. I practiced my pliés all that week with my little pug in my arms. After all she was my first real dancing partner.

A World More Real than Real

In a summer that began with little promise of being very special, something extraordinary happened. My dream became real, and I wrapped myself in the world of ballet.

The temperature continued to soar in the 90s, but I hardly noticed the heat. Every Monday, Wednesday, and Friday morning I ran down Main Street to get to my dance class. Dashing up the long staircase was a perfect warm up for the strenuous lesson ahead.

In a room even the air-conditioner found difficult to keep cool, and my face covered with perspiration, I worked hard to meet Miss Hanson's expectations. Each lesson brought me closer to fulfilling my dream.

"Plié __down___ One, two, three, four."

"Up___ One, two, three, four."

With each gentle tap on my shoulder to straighten my back and hold my head high, my pliés improved. Miss Hanson was a good teacher. I liked her so much.

"Pirouettes, please. Keep your eye on a spot on the wall, Sarah." When I fell on my rump, I remembered Aunt May's words, "Some days I would stay working on my pirouettes until bands of red and orange ribboned the sky, and the moon lighted my way home. Would you be willing to work that hard, Sarah?" Then I would just get up and try again.

Miss Hanson always wore a short wrap-around skirt over her leotard. When she turned, her skirt swirled gracefully around her hips. Someday I was going to have a skirt like that, I thought. Maybe I'd even teach ballet. I admired Miss Hanson very much.

Friday afternoon one week after my first lesson, I was sitting on the patio trying to read *The Call of the Wild*. The only sound was a bee buzzing around a yellow rose. Focusing on Buck's horrific journey from the sun-kissed valley in California to the Arctic darkness was difficult. I didn't want the dog's pain to sully my world where everything was so beautiful and so right. My mind wandered back to the beam of sunlight on my feet in class as I rose up and down in relevé.

Mom started to take my dream of becoming a ballerina more seriously. When I returned after class, my face glowing,

I could see she was pleased.

I had been wearing tights and a tee shirt, and it didn't bother me at all. When I arrived home from class on the Friday of the second week, there was a pink tote bag on my bed. In the bag were two leotards, one the palest of pink and the other black, with matching tights and ballet slippers. On the cover of the card tucked in one of the slippers was a painting of *The Star* by Degas. Surrounded by a puff of pink tulle, the ballerina was balancing in an elegant pose on one leg. Through the magic of footlights, her cheeks glowed, and the expression on her face captured the joy of dance. I read the note and wanted to hold on to my happiness forever.

> "We want you to become the very best ballerina you can, Dancing Feet."

> Love,

> Mom and Dad.

My dream had become their dream for me now. I ran into the kitchen and held them close.

When Aunt May returned from Europe, I told her everything, and it didn't surprise me at all that my aunt's birthday gift that year was a framed print of the *Ballet at the Paris Opera* now on the wall above my desk. I often look at the painting and remember the magic of that summer when the dream I had since I was a little girl became real.

Aunt May always supported my dream. One night with the stars out of hiding and the wind caressing the tall oaks, Isabella and I were sitting out on the patio listening to the whispering leaves. When my aunt arrived, she had a book in her arms with a ballerina on the cover posed gracefully on pointe in an ankle length tutu. "Sarah, I think you're ready to read *Apollo Angels.* I underlined some passages I know you'll find very interesting."

"Apollo angels. What a lovely title, Aunt May."

I went to bed early that night. When I placed the book of the angel on pointe on my night table, the lamp sent a ring of light shining on the ballerina posed gracefully. I fell asleep and dreamed my favorite dream. I had been having wonderful dreams almost every night since I started ballet lessons.

> *In a circle of light*
> *A ballerina dances*
> *To the rustling of leaves*
> *And the sound of the wind chime*
> *Swaying on the branch of the kwanzan tree.*

The next day Isabella and I sat under the maple tree, the same tree where Patty and I sat on the day my dream of becoming a ballerina first began to be real. When I started to read the book, one of the passages my aunt underlined really reached out to me. I read the passage several times.

"Ballet brings you to **a spiritual world more real than real**," the famous choreographer George Balanchine had said. "In order for a dancer to reach this level of awareness, she first has to know exactly why she does a tendu this way and not that way. This requires self-awareness, clarity, and training."

A spiritual world more real than real. The words kept repeating in my head. I felt like the ballerina in my dreams rising up on pointe to reach the stars and the moon.

Today *Apollo's Angels* stands on my desk bookended by my bronzed toe shoes, the pointe slippers I wore the day I danced the Sugar Plum Fairy. When I look through the book and remember, a single tear rolls down my cheek

After my ballet class that summer, Patty and I would stop for a yogurt before going to the high school for our swimming lessons. By the end of the summer, we had overcome our fear of jumping off the springboard 10 feet above the deep end of the pool and received certificates of excellence for our diving ability.

Patty's framed Merit Award had a prominent place on the wall in her room. I tucked my certificate in my desk drawer under Aunt May's ballerina poems. Although I was proud of learning to dive, ballet had become my first love.

I began keeping a dance journal. When I read the journal today, I can still feel the magic in the moment.

Monday, July 6th

The summer is hot, but even as the rhododendron leaves turn yellow, I welcomed the sun slanting across the studio this morning. With the radiant light shining on my face, I felt like *The Star* in Degas's painting. I remember through the magic of footlights, her cheeks glowed, and the expression on her face captured the joy of dance. I love ballet so much.

After class. I practiced my relevé on the patio to the tempo of Isabella's short, high barks.

Wednesday, July 8th

"Flex, point, flex, point even at home. It helps strengthen your arches," Miss Hanson said. While I read *The Call of the Wild*, I flexed and pointed my feet at least 20 times. Poor Buck, what a terrible situation he's in. I only read two pages tonight, but Mom says there's no reason I shouldn't keep up with my reading. She left *Little Women* on my desk. Maybe I'll start that tomorrow.

Friday, July 10th

Nature danced with me tonight. As I balancéd to the rhythm of the cicadas - clickity click, clickity click – a thrush trilled its song on the top limb of the birch.

Monday, July 13th

Today Aunt May gave me a notebook with a picture of Degas's *Ballet at the Paris Opera* on the cover. On the first page she wrote, "Sarah, maybe you'll write a story someday about a girl who has a dream of becoming a ballerina."

Wednesday, July 15th

When I practiced my jetés across the lawn before going to class, the squirrels joined in high-flying leaps from the oak to the hickory tree. We made a grand corps de ballet. Miss H said my jetés were very good. When I got home, I told my fleet-footed friends.

Friday, July 17th

In class the raindrops pitter-pattered on the window pane in unison to Soren Bebe's lovely piano pieces. Suddenly the gray day became bright again.

Monday, July 20th

Isabella and I still begin our day with yoga. Today Miss Hanson asked me to tell the class how yoga can help them. I told them my aunt said yoga is a great way to stretch and strengthen your body, focus your mind, and help you remain calm. After class Betsy said she was going to do yoga every morning now. Betsy and I have become good friends.

Wednesday, July 22nd

In challenging moments when I struggle with my pirouettes and my knees ache and my arms feel heavy, I still know ballet is what I want to do most.

Friday, July 24th

As we listened to the music of *La Bayadere,* a word that sounds like buy a deer, Miss H told us the story of the ballet. She said the bayadere was a dancing girl in the Hindu temple sworn to love her handsome warrior forever. Doomed by the gods, the lovers were separated and only in death were reunited in eternal love. In this exotic ballet set in Ancient India, the lovely bayadere performs many triple pirouettes, Miss H said. We worked on our pirouettes most of the class. I found pirouettes difficult to do today, so I practiced them out on the patio before I went to bed. One evening star illuminated the sky, and I made a wish: "Star light, star bright, help me with my pirouettes tonight."

Monday, July 27th

I had a wonderful dream last night.

> *The curtain rises,*
>
> *And in radiant ring of light*
>
> *A temple maiden pirouettes.*

Waking up before the birds began to sing, I quivered with

the memory of the temple maiden in my dream and felt every turn she made. Isabella and I went out to the garden and I picked a lavender tulip and two golden daffodils for Mom.

Wednesday, July 29th

I practiced my sauté tonight. As I jumped up from first position, I remember The Dance of the Flowers the summer I was eight and wanted so much to be a ballerina. Now dancing beneath the stars accompanied by the song of three robins and a cello-throated dove, I really feel like a ballerina. Miss Hanson's a wonderful teacher.

In the middle of August, I started taking classes on Saturdays. After my lesson the dance studio rang with the laughter of Miss Hanson's youngest students. I loved watching Miss H teach the young dancers. She was firm but gentle, and they loved her very much.

"Chin up. That's perfect Carolyn."

"Back straight and knees bent. Good job, Robert."

"Danielle, your pointed toes look so lovely in your new ballet slippers."

"Tommy, let's work on your jetés today."

While Miss Hanson worked with the dancers individually in preparation for their Christmas recital, I gathered my young friends around me on the floor in her office. "Storytime, kids."

Waving the shiny black notebook with my name in big bold letters on the cover always brought a round of cheers.

"Is the story about a little pug, Sarah?

"Tommy, this story is about a very courageous little pug."

The Terror in the Night

In the dark and empty roads of a faraway village of long ago, Samara roams alone. The courageous pug has left family and friends to face a gruesome monster who threatens the people in this peaceful hamlet.

What's a hamlet, Sarah?"

"It's a small village, Robert."

The fire-breathing demon has filled the minds and the hearts of the villagers with fear. It is said that at night the evil beast remains in his cave, and a long darkness descends. When the beast flies through the air at dawn, his fiery breath brings day, but the villagers are still afraid.

On the darkest night of the year the valiant pug travels deep into the dense forest to find the firedrake.

"What's a firedrake, Sarah?"

"It's another name for dragon, Carolyn." I was always pleased when my young friends asked questions.

Suddenly horrific wails echo in the starless night, and the ground begins to shake. The evil monster is near. Samara follows the sound to a hollow in the mountain. The little pug is brave.

As he enters the cave, the frightful shrieks grow louder. Emboldened by his desire to help the people of the village, Samara walks without fear to the deepest part of the cavern where a fiery light emanates.

"Does emboldened mean he is courageous, Sarah?"

"Yes, Tommy." Tommy was a smart little boy and the oldest in the class.

When the fearless pug's eyes adjust to the raging light emanating from the dragon's fiery breath, he sees the sharp-eyed dragon that strikes terror into the people of this small village. The firedrake has a humongous green scaly body and a long-barbed tail, but Samara is not afraid.

He speaks to the evil monster. "Why do you bring such dread into the hearts of the gentle people in this village. They have done you no harm." In the silent moments before the dragon speaks, the brave pug shows no fear.

Then the dragon speaks. "The people of the village do not understand. They believe I am a force of evil. But even from my cave in the long, dark of winter, I tell the wind not to be harsh. Then as winter departs and nature awakens, I fly across their fields. My outstretched wings shining like stained-glass in the sun banish the darkness. The days grow long and the rain falls lightly to nourish their plants.

All summer I inspire the villagers to plant pink and white peonies and roses of every color in their gardens and to appreciate the natural beauty around them. But they are still afraid. They do not understand that the energy flowing from my fiery breath brings beauty to their land. It is this vital energy that encourages the villagers to act in harmony with each other and their environment, to work hard, to grow vegetables in abundance, and to eat wholesome food."

It is true, Samara thinks. Even as the people show great fear, the village has thrived. It has been said that in springtime peach blossoms flourish bearing delicious fruit. In every season there is something in bloom surrounding them in nature's beauty. The grass is green and lush well into winter, and crops are plentiful through most of the year.

Encouraged by the dragon's words, Samara leaves the cave to tell the villagers what he has seen and what he has heard. He hopes the gentle giant's message will banish their fear and fill their minds with good thoughts.

When Samara tells the people of the village the dragon's benevolent words, they know the pug speaks truths. Their rice fields have flourished, their gardens produce beautiful flowers, and the sea provides them with a bounty of fish. Now they will welcome the rain, a gift from the caring firedrake to help their crops grow. And when the sun grows strong, they will give thanks to the dragon for helping their flowers to bloom.

Even today many, many years later the dragon's words stir the imagination of the villagers, and his message has spread to many surrounding villages. To honor the caring dragon with a long-barbed tail, the people spread seeds for the birds and do no harm to any living creature.

The gentle green serpent sends his message to you and to me, my dancing friends, "Let the dragon move each of us to do good in the world." The children nod their heads.

"I promise I'll care for the flowers and the birds and all living things," Alice says.

"I'm going to help my mom with the compost heap." Robert was so caring. When the children left their clothes on the locker floor, he always folded them and put them on the bench.

"What's a compost heap, Bobby?" Deborah was always so eager to learn.

"It's a mound of food scraps like egg shells and orange peels and coffee grinds that my mom piles up in our backyard. After a while the garbage turns into fertile soil for her to spread around and help her flowers to grow, Debbie."

"And I'm never going to be afraid of the strange shadows

on the walls in my bedroom at night anymore. It's just the firedrake watching over me."

"That's right, Tommy. A man as wise as the dragon once said that we have the power to look deep into our fears, and then our fear will not rule us." Since Tommy was the oldest, I knew he would understand.

"Is Isabella as brave as Samara, Sarah?"

"Of course she is, Tommy. Maybe I'll bring my little pug to visit you, but don't tell Miss H," I whispered as the children returned to class.

I remember the gleam in their eyes barely hid the secret they shared—they were going to meet Miss Isabella. I loved reading my stories to my young dancing friends.

The summer flew by too quickly, but the flock of migrating geese and rustle of crisp leaves on my walks with Isabella didn't disturb me at all. It was just the beginning. Mom said I could continue taking lessons in the fall as long as they didn't interfere with my school work.

Elegance and Grace

When the air turned crisp and Tchaikovsky's *Nutcracker Suite* filled the studio, I had a dream every night. The same dream I had when I was four years old.

Surrounded by the sound of bells in a majestic forest
Filled with candied sweets and crystal snowflakes,
A little ballerina sweeps into view.

Beneath trees with snow-rimmed limbs
Glittering in the moon's light,
She moves like the wind

Each night the dream made me strong as I prepared my role as the Sugar Plum Fairy for our winter recital. The feeling of joy could have sent me to the moon. I was the Sugar Plum Fairy who had been so much a part of my life since I was a little girl.

On opening night, I stood in the wings watching my classmates sweep across the stage to the one-two-three beat of "The Waltz of the Flowers." Everything appeared like a treasured photograph. *The Nutcracker* ballet I saw when I was seven years old was still a vivid memory. When the ballerinas billowing pink gowns unfurled like the petals of a rose even the air held a fragrance.

Betsy danced beautifully. The elegant Dewdrop bound across the stage in a flurry of jetés and pirouettes to join the circle of waltzing flowers, her forward leaps and spins dissolving the air.

Then, propelled by the sound of heavenly bells, I rose up on my toes, and something magical happened. All my fear of performing on pointe for the very first time disappeared, and I became the ballerina in my dream. My arabesques were steady, my jetés high and long, and I didn't have any problem with my pirouettes. I could see Miss Hanson standing in the wings smiling.

With "Brava. Brava" still ringing in my ears, I ran up to Mom after the performance. "How was I, Mom?"

"Sarah, you danced like an angel. I'm so proud of you."

Dad hugged me so tightly I thought I would break, and Aunt May just bubbled with enthusiasm. "Wonderful! Wonderful! Wonderful, Sarah!"

"You were the best dancer in the whole ballet," Patty said. "I wish Barbara could have come." Barbara had been in bed all week with the flu.

At home in the light of the cold winter moon, I picked up Isabella and we danced around my room. "Oh, Monkey Face, I wish you were there. It was just so grand."

"Please try to go to sleep, Sarah. We promised to have brunch with Aunt May. She has a surprise for her favorite ballerina."

Since I was a toddler, Aunt May had written me poems to keep my ballerina dream alive. While I lay in bed trying to fall asleep, Isabella curled up by my side, I took out my memory box and read the poems to Miss Iz.

For Sarah on her Seventh Birthday
Beneath the purple-blue blossom
On the hibiscus tree,
I see my ballerina
Spinning and leaping,
Enchanting me with her elegance and grace.

When I read Isabella her favorite poem,

For Sarah and a pug named Isabella.
With the moon shining silver
On her fawn coat of fur

A little pug dances by a young girl's side.
In the light of the moon,
The puppy and the ballerina
Create a glorious pas de deux.

she fell asleep quickly, a moonbeam turning her coat of fur silver. As the night sky became light and the morning star rose, I finally fell asleep. In that time between night and day, a light snow had fallen. With the memory of my performance still so vivid, I opened my eyes and all the world was right. The sun shone brightly, the snow-rimmed limbs of every tree glistened, and a brilliant red cardinal perched on a branch of the kwanzan tree.

At brunch my aunt placed four tickets into my hand. "We're going to see *Sleeping Beauty* next Sunday. Ask Patty and Barbara and Betsy to join us, Sarah. When I was your age, I loved this beautiful ballet and still do. You know Tchaikovsky's marvelous music so well. Mom tells me you play the CD all the time."

Isabella and I grew up dancing to the music from *Sleeping Beauty,* and I couldn't think of a ballet I wanted to see more. "Oh, Aunt May, that's wonderful. Patty and Barbara have never seen a ballet, and Betsy only saw *The Nutcracker* in the movies last year. They'll be so excited to see a ballet on the stage."

Sundays are always special, but even the birds were celebrating the Sunday we went to see *Sleeping Beauty*. I remember I woke up to a chorus of sparrows in the kwanzan tree.

I immediately put on my CD of Tchaikovsky's *Sleeping Beauty*. I had been playing it all week to make the waiting go quickly. Awakened by the glorious music, Isabella dashed over. Holding her up by her front paws, Monkey Face and I began our day with a delightful pas de deux. My friends arrived to the gentle melody of the harp in the opening of the Rose Adagio.

"I just love Tchaikovsky, Sarah." Betsy twirled gracefully down the hall. "Hi, Mrs. Baker."

"Sit down and have some pancakes girls." Mom's delicious pancakes never tasted so good. When Aunt May arrived, we put our arms around her and wrapped her in our happiness.

"Thanks, girls. Now let's go and make wonderful memories."

In the lobby of the theater Princess Aurora was performing the Rose Adagio on a large TV screen. "Look at her arabesque, Sarah. Her extended leg is in a straight line with her supporting leg." That day Betsy and I watched each dancer with the dream of becoming "prima" ballerinas.

Patty's eyes opened wide. "How can she turn around so many times without falling?" I remember Patty had fallen several times while rehearsing The Dance of the Flowers that summer when I was still hoping that my dream of becoming a ballerina would come true.

"What a fabulous costume! How can she stand on her toes like that?" Barbara who was not easily impressed found everything amazing that day.

"The house is now open." When we entered the auditorium, a little girl dancing up and down the center aisle in her ballet slippers made me smile. Not so long ago I was that little girl. The red velvet seats seemed larger then, but the brilliant crystal chandelier and luxurious gold curtain were the same as they waited for the magic to begin.

"Welcome, Ladies." The usher smiled as she handed us our playbills. "Do you girls study ballet?"

"Yes," I answered enthusiastically. The thought always made me happy.

On the cover of the playbill a ballerina slept peacefully with her feet poised in pink toe slippers. I put the program carefully in my tote to save in my memory box. The Christmas my dream of becoming a ballerina was just a tiny seed waiting to grow, Aunt May had given me a music box with a ballerina twirling on top. I saved the box it came in, and it now holds a treasure of ballet memories stored safely under my bed.

My Little Golden Book of *Sleeping Beauty* still sits on the top shelf of my bookcase with *Ella Bella Ballerina* and *Tallulah's Tutu,* but revisiting the magical kingdom in a glorious ballet was beyond my expectations. The *Nutcracker* at seven was magical. I will always remember it as **the place where my dreams lived.** But now I knew so much more and was really able to appreciate the ballet. The best part of writing is remembering, and I'm reliving the moment now.

When the conductor raises his baton and the auditorium resounds with Tchaikovsky's music, I have to struggle to keep my feet still. The gold curtain rises slowly unveiling a lavish gilded palace hall. The audience sighs. A grand christening celebration honoring the birth of the King and Queen's first child fills the stage with all the grandeur of once upon a time. Fairies in billowing tutus of pink and yellow and blue dance around the cradle presenting gifts of beauty and courage and kindheartedness.

Then with the swiftness of a solar eclipse, the golden moment turns dark. Arriving in a carriage pulled by grotesque, bug-like creatures, the wicked Carabosse cloaked all in black leaps from the coach jabbing her arms in the air. She's furious. She hasn't been invited to the jubilee and vows revenge. Princess Aurora will prick her finger and die on her sixteenth birthday.

The years go by quickly, and the curtain rises once again on a magnificent celebration. Children, many children, circle round and round swinging garlands of flowers over their heads.

It's Princess Aurora's sixteenth birthday, and princes from around the world have come to ask for her hand in marriage. In a shimmering pink tutu, the lovely Aurora sweeps onto the stage like a sunburst at dawn. In a grand gesture to win her heart, the noblemen offer the princess a rose. The music builds, and Aurora, balancing perfectly in unsupported arabesques, takes the rose from each prince's hand. I feel every movement, the extension of her leg, the curve of her spine, and the tilt of her head. I whisper to Aunt May, "Do you think I'll ever be able to do an arabesque like that?" A simple nod of her head was so reassuring. Aunt May always encouraged my dream of becoming a "prima" ballerina.

Without warning, darkness descends. A stranger appears carrying a spindle. It's the malevolent Carabosse. Aurora takes the spindle, pricks her finger, and collapses under the evil one's curse.

But the wicked Carabosse has failed to achieve revenge. Glimmering in lavender tulle, the benevolent Lilac fairy pirouettes and grands jetés, casting her powerful spell. Princess Aurora and the entire kingdom will sleep for a very long time hidden behind thorny thistles and tangles of prickly shrubs.

One hundred years pass. Prince Désirée sweeps across the stage in a mastery of twirls and grands jetés. When he sees the beautiful Aurora, he awakens her with a kiss.

Love triumphs and a grand wedding celebration takes place. At the gala all the fantastic characters from my childhood fairy tales perform lively dances. It doesn't seem so long ago when I was sitting on Mom's lap while she read me Cinderella and Little Red Riding Hood and the Big Bad Wolf. That day Puss n' Boots and the White Cat really captured the fun in dance.

Then with the speed of a bolt of lightning, Charmant, a prince who has been transformed into a bird for falling in love with the beautiful Florine, soars across the stage to the bird-like melody of a flute. Fluttering his arms, the majestic blue bird springs up in an explosion of leaps. Crossing his feet and beating his legs like hummingbird's wings, his arms span out like an eagle in flight.

"Aunt May," I whisper, "The bluebird can really fly." Aunt May just nods her head.

In a spectacular pas de deux, the Bluebird reunites with his beautiful Florine and LOVE triumphs again.

"Bravo. Bravo."

Then with striking arabesques and rapid pirouettes Princess Aurora joins Prince Desirée in a grand pas de deux. "Watch for the fish dive, girls." Aunt May whispers.

In a final expression of LOVE, Aurora dives in an elegant leap into her handsome prince's arms. Raising her legs high like the curved tail of a mermaid swooping over the crest of a wave, Aurora balances gracefully on her prince's leg.

"Brava. Brava."

In JOY and all the splendor and magic of once upon the time, the entire kingdom joins in dance, and the lovely princess and her handsome prince live in happiness ever after.

"Bravo. Bravo."

The little girl sitting next to me leaped up. "This is the best ballet I ever saw in the whole wide world." I felt the same. I turned to my aunt and gave her a hug.

"Aunt May, this fairy tale will remain with me always as a glorious, breathtaking ballet. Forever. Always. I love you so much."

"Isn't it wonderful, Sarah, what dancers can do? Remember the words I underlined in *Apollo's Angels* – dancers require 'self-awareness, clarity, and training' then they are able to rise above gravity and dance like the flying bluebird."

Aunt May always kept my ballerina dream real.

"Gosh! I don't think I've ever seen anything so beautiful. Not ever." Barbara's enthusiasm surprised us all.

Betsy didn't say a word and I understood. She never wanted the moment to end.

"Aunt May, I loved every minute of the ballet."

"I'm so glad, Patty. We'll all go to see *Swan Lake* in the Spring. Promise. Once more we wrapped my aunt in our happiness.

Even though I'm traveling a different path today, this enchanting ballet will always have a special place in my heart. Betsy and I go to the ballet several times a year, and *Sleeping Beauty* is always on our list.

In the spring as I prepared for my performance in *Les Sylphides,* I wrote in my journal, "Miss H wants us to dance the ballet in a graceful kaleidoscope of movements in perfect harmony with Chopin's beautiful music. A poetry of elegant form," she said.

Then in a mid-summer night, the moon shining bright through a filigree of leaves, six butterfly wingéd ballerinas in billowing white gowns pas de bourrée onto the stage. Lifting **my arms** to reach beyond the trees and over the clouds, I feel that I'm dancing in a dream. My legs move forward and back, forward and back skimming the stage like a current of warm air. Every step bringing me closer to fulfilling my dream of becoming a "prima" ballerina.

I know we met Miss H's expectations that day. Standing in the wings, her radiant smile expressed how pleased she was.

Even today I love playing my CD of *Les Sylphides* and living the enchantment in this moment again. The memory always comes trailing a fragrant scent. After the performance Mom came back stage, the pink roses in her arms reflecting in her eyes. "Sarah, you danced beautifully. I'm so proud of you."

Aunt May grabbed me and kissed both cheeks. "Sarah, we're living our dream."

On the drive home I traveled back with Dad to that frosty day in December, the day when the seed of my ballerina dream began to grow.

"Sarah, do you remember that cold, blustery day you swept into the house looking as if you just arrived from an arctic tundra and announced, **'Daddy, I'm going to be a ballerina someday?"** Well, I guess wishes really do come true. You danced like an angel tonight, Dancing Feet." I sighed. I loved ballet so much.

In the fall family and friends gathered at my house to watch me on TV in *The Little Match Girl.*

Two minutes, Miss Baker." Miss H bends down and adjusts

the ribbons on my pointe slippers. "You're going to do a great job today, Sarah."

"One minute, Miss Baker." Miss H and I walk hand in hand to the small stage. The red light on the TV camera flashing just a few feet away. I breathe deeply, and then the calm.

It's the eve before Christmas. There are no stars in the sky. A small red brick house sheds the only light on an empty street.

A little match girl gazes longingly through the lacey patterns frosting the window pane. A yule log blazes on an open hearth trimmed with fir garlands and red velvet bows. Silver bowls overflow with candy canes and marzipan reindeers. Under a Christmas tree radiant with candlelight, gifts wrapped in shiny gold paper wait for the arrival of Christmas morning. Lorna and Betsy and Barry dance around the glimmering tree.

In the glow of the candlelight, the match girl forgets her hunger and cold. But the hundreds of candles on the evergreen are unable to share their warmth with the shivering waif. Her dress tattered, her shoes worn, and flakes of snow covering her long brown hair, **I rise up** on pointe. My whole body in harmony with the music of Saint- Saens. I dared to dream,

> *A star falls silently from the sky*
> *And touches a ballerina's heart.*

> *Rising on pointe*
> *Her arms lift high*
> *Reaching for moon.*

and somewhere over the rainbow my dream came true.

As I pirouette, my tattered dress wraps around my legs struggling to keep warm. A cold wind blows, and snowflakes, silvery-white in the candlelight, make no excuse for continuing to fall. I curl up on the doorstep and draw my legs close to keep out the wind. An icy frost bites my hands. I light my matchsticks to send away the cold. With each flickering flame the night becomes brighter than day, and I arrive at that special place **where dreams live.**

In the first brilliant flame children dance in red velvet frocks. I join the children in balancés. The vision fades. I strike another match. Berries and big green pears surround a succulent roast goose waiting on a silver plate for the feast to begin. I jeté and pirouette gleefully around the scrumptious fare. In the fiery glow from my last matchstick, there are gifts with big gold bows under a giant spruce more beautiful than any I have ever seen. The tree is tall and thousands of candles like stars in the sky burn on each lush, green limb. I pas de bourreé and arabesque and pirouette as I reach for the radiance of each flickering flame. Then springing into my final grand jeté, I collapse to the floor. No cold, no hunger to harm me now. The only sound is my heart pounding, and my classmates clapping softly in the wings.

When I arrived home, Dad was the first to greet me. "Sarah, you danced like a sylph with angel's wings." Angel's wings. I remembered *Apollo's Angels,* and Mr. Balanchine's words repeat in my head, ballet requires "self-awareness, clarity, and training," he said. My hard work had given me my reward.

Mom found it difficult to put into words how proud she was when **A Bright Star: Introducing Sarah Baker** appeared in bold letters on the TV screen. Family and friends raised their glasses, "To our lovely match girl and our brightest star.

The Rose Fades

The prince offers Aurora a rose.
Balancing perfectly in unsupported arabesques,
The princess takes the rose from the nobleman.

Am I awake or is this a dream? Am I really dancing the magnificent Rose Adagio in Tchaikovsky's *Sleeping Beauty*? My hours of practice convince me this is real.

I rise up on pointe. My toe slippers stealing the glow from the footlights in every joyful step, my body moving in harmony with the beautiful music. I pirouette. In this moment I hear Mr. Balanchine's words again, **"Ballet brings you to a spiritual world more real than real."**

Filled with the joy of dance, I stand before each prince in an unsupported arabesque to accept a rose. I struggle to keep my balance. The music rises to steady my hand. When I soar across the stage in my final grand jeté, something marvelous happens. My dream to be a **prima** ballerina is closer than it has ever been.

After the performance Aunt May says the magic words, "Sarah, my love, you danced like a **prima ballerina** tonight."

Then very soon the light went out, and the dark place was so scary. I remember when my dream of becoming a ballerina became real, I had thought that nothing bad could ever happen to me now, but I was wrong. Isabella was only ten years old when she became very ill.

Since my little pug was a puppy, we took long walks together. In early spring when the daffodils were in bloom, she delighted in their fragrance and pressed her nose to each blossom dancing in the March wind. In summer she always stopped to sniff Mrs. Warren's fragrant roses flourishing in the sun. In fall she lingered before a crimson mum or even a single green leaf, holding its place proudly on the rhododendron bush. She delighted in the natural beauty around her.

But when fall arrived that year Isabella wasn't running through the pachysandra and crisp fallen leaves. She had no interest in smelling the earthy scents of the chrysanthemums surrounding our home. From my bed at night, I could hear her in the kitchen slurping the water in her bowl. In the morning there was no puppy dog pose to wake me up, and her cute monkey face didn't greet me with enthusiastic lollypop-licks when I came home from school. She was usually taking a nap. Even the sound of Tchaikovsky's glorious *Nutcracker* or *Sleeping Beauty* didn't bring her to my side. My favorite dancing partner never wanted to dance anymore.

Most of the day she just curled up in her bed. Eyes closed. Breathing heavily. Several times during the day she stood near the refrigerator and barked. Although I enjoyed giving Isabella treats, carrots and celery and slices of crisp apples, I wondered why she was hungry all the time. The hearty bowl of kibble with chunks of roasted chicken didn't satisfy her anymore, and she looked a little thinner every day.

Saturday, September 20th is still so clear in my mind. That day it became very obvious that Isabella was ill. The morning was warmed by a bright sun, and we went for an early walk before I left for my dance class. As we passed Mrs. Warren tending her roses, she stopped weeding. "Isabella's so thin. Isn't she feeling well?"

"She's OK," I said quickly. But seeing Isabella through Mrs. Warren's eyes was the final awakening. I picked her up in my arms and ran home. "Mom, I don't think Isabella's well. Even Mrs. Warren noticed how thin she's gotten."

Although we all saw that Isabella had lost her sparkle and was losing weight, Mom often just commented, "I guess our little pug's not a puppy anymore." But that day Mom immediately called Dr. J.

Dr. J recognized her symptoms. "Bring Isabella in this afternoon, Mrs. Baker, and I'll take a series of blood tests."

When I went to my dance class that day, my heart was heavy.

"Sarah, are you feeling ill?"

"I'm OK, Miss H." But I wasn't. For days I waited anxiously for the result of the blood tests, and my heart skipped a beat every time the phone rang. Three days later, rain all day, the phone rang in the late afternoon. I could hear Dr. J's deep voice. "Mrs. Baker, Isabella has diabetes, but with a good diet, exercise, and daily insulin injections she'll be fine."

Suddenly the rain stopped, and the sun came out. With proper care Isabella would be fine. No more sweet treats for Iz, that's for sure.

Twice a day Mom or Dad gave Isabella an insulin injection which Monkey Face didn't mind at all, and my favorite dancing partner was back. When I played *Sleeping Beauty,* she was by my side jumping as high as a jack rabbit. We danced every day and took long walks before I left for school or my ballet lessons. Bursting with energy, her eyes sparkling, her quick stride only interrupted to stop to smell a rose or a leaf. One morning we passed Mrs. Warren house, and she called from her window, "Isabella's feeling better, I see."

That fall every chrysanthemum made me happy as I watched my little pug press her nose to the bounty of golden blossoms around our home. In winter when a light snow fell, she even danced with me on the patio. Isabella was back. I now know this dark moment was preparing me for what was to come.

While still in the glow of my Rose Adagio and TV debut and with Isabella doing so well, I began preparing for my role of Odette in the winter recital of *Swan Lake.*

One evening, stars lighting a lilac sky, I had just finished a three-hour class and stayed to practice my tour jetés. I liked the quiet in the studio at dusk. When I made my first high turning leap, I hit the floor with a sickening thump. My knee popped, and all the air was knocked out of my lungs.

What happened next has become a blur. The ligament in my right leg had been completely torn, Dr. Braun said. The official diagnosis was ACL, a torn anterior cruciate ligament. Miss H had warned me so many times, "Land in a plié, Sarah, to cushion your knees."

"Perhaps after surgery and a period of physical therapy, you could return to dancing," Dr Braun held my hand, his eyes expressing deep concern, "but you'll probably be anxious with every step that requires landing and pivoting, and there's no guarantee the accident couldn't happen again. Sarah, you're young, only at the beginning of a dancing career. There's so much a girl with your imagination can do. Your mother tells me you're a talented writer. I'm sorry but I have to recommend that you give up your dream of becoming a ballerina."

Abandon my dream! Grandpa's words to Aunt May resounded in my head. I couldn't believe Dr. Braun was saying them to me.

"But Mom, it's not fair. It's not fair at all," I remember crying out at Dr. Braun's devastating recommendation. I wanted to roll back the clock and take the nightmare away. My imagination wouldn't allow this reality in. I saw myself leaping over the wind-swept snow mounds like a squirrel jumping from tree to tree, and I wanted more than anything to be that little girl again. To be where my dream first began.

My world collapsed. My dream had faded like the morning mist, and no sun followed. Each morning I woke up and the nightmare was there. The dream I had for as long as I could remember had been shattered, and "all the king's horses and all the king's men" couldn't put it back together again.

For weeks I stayed in my room. When Dad heard me crying, he came in and wrapped me in his arms. His heart was also broken.

Mom couldn't talk to me without filling up with tears, and day after day my little pug lay quietly by my side on the bed.

Whimpering softly, her big brown eyes expressed compassion, but even on nights when the moon shone bright, there was no sparkle in them.

Aunt May was in as much pain as I was. In the years I had been taking lessons, I was fulfilling her dream as well. Every day she visited, and we read together. At the end of *A Tree Grows in Brooklyn,* we cried.

Francie Nolan "looked down into the yard. The tree whose leaf umbrellas had curled around, under and over her fire escape had been cut down . . . But the tree hadn't died. . . a NEW tree had grown from the stump . . . and started to grow towards the sky again."

I knew I had to begin again, but I wasn't ready for NEW beginnings, and my aunt understood. We just held each other, and I repeated my excruciating cry, "It's not fair, Aunt May. It's not fair at all."

Then came the quiet. The roses bloomed and the birds sang their songs and the wind chime murmured a delicate melody, but I refused to receive the comfort nature offered. Even though family and friends supported me in every way, I felt so alone, alone with only my memories.

"Let's have a barbecue, Sarah. We'll invite Betsy and Patty and Barbara." Dad tried his best to bring back my smile.

"No thanks, Dad."

"Sarah, get your camera. The peony looks so beautiful in the golden light of the afternoon sun."

"Not now, Mom."

"Would you like to sit out on the patio and read *Little Women*?"

"Not today, Mom." When ballet was the center of my life, I had put off reading *Little Women*. Now the book had become a painful reminder of what I had then.

"Why don't you take Isabella for a walk?"

"I'm too tired right now, Mom."

Patty came every day and without saying a word just placed a tiny bouquet of lilacs from her garden on my lap. I always asked Mom to take them into the kitchen.

Barbara brought Ariel. Even when the kitten looked at me with eyes as bright as emeralds, she couldn't banish the darkness in my heart.

Betsy called every evening before she went to bed, and the sadness in her voice made me even sadder. I felt the pain in my heart was never going to end.

Then the anger. The Christmas holidays arrived, and I refused to allow Mom and Dad to put up a Christmas tree. When the doorbell rang on Christmas eve, Barbara's cheery

Merry Christmas as she handed me a lovely poinsettia just made me feel worse. "Thanks, Barbara." I didn't even ask her in.

I really didn't understand that my family and friends were feeling my pain. That winter the temperature fell into the teens almost every day. Standing at the kitchen window looking out into the limpid winter light, my heart felt as frozen as the layer of ice covering the patio table.

Day faded into night. Night into day. And the seasons changed. The sound of the fallen acorns announcing the end of summer embraced the melancholy I was feeling. When school began, I didn't want to be with my friends.

"Let's go for a coke, Sarah?"

"Not today, Patty, I have to go to physical therapy." I still hadn't decided what I was going to do, and the therapy was going very slowly. The idea that I could return to the world of ballet grew dimmer each day. Mom's words kept repeating in my head, "You're sensible, Sarah. I know you'll do the right thing."

When Spring arrived and the air exploded with the sweet scent of peonies, returning to dance classes wasn't likely to happen very soon. As the cherry blossoms burst into bloom, I just moped around the house playing Tchaikovsky's *Sleeping Beauty* and *Swan Lake* over and over.

When the morning mist vanished in the sun's rays, my loneliness lingered even as the sun grew strong and shed its golden light on the roses, beautiful and bountiful that spring. Nature was no longer my friend. Dr. Braun's words were always there. "Your ligament has been completely torn, Sarah. I have to recommend you stop ballet."

The temperature in May was pleasant enough that year. One evening at twilight I wandered across the lawn. The stillness broken by a light breeze. I quivered a sob of pity for myself. If I couldn't be a ballerina, I didn't know who I was. The soft wind and the dwindling light were in sympathy with me.

That night Nature nourished my loneliness. The insects buzzed rhythmically, and the trees sang a doleful song. As night fell, sadness creeped in and gained strength, and there was no shining star to guide my way.

Even on evenings when the lingering light of a radiant sunset yielded to the night sky and stars clustered around a thin crescent moon, I refused to enjoy the beauty surrounding me. Returning to my room, I listened to *Sleeping Beauty*. Only Tchaikovsky's music could fill the empty space in my heart. Each precious moment of my Rose Adagio still vivid, I often fell asleep with an imaginary rose pressed to my heart. The single red rose in my imagination was more real than the host of golden daffodils dancing in the gentle breeze outside my bedroom window.

On wet afternoons I welcomed the rain and walked beneath dark clouds waiting for the rain drops and my tears to become friends. In the barren winter that followed, many times I just stood at the window staring at the bare tree branches swaying in the wind. They reminded me of ballerinas, and tears flowed down my cheeks.

As the days grew warm and the sun shone bright, the butterflies returned. But the monarchs fluttering around the host of golden daffodils didn't interest me at all.

"Sarah, the hosta is coming up so lush this year," Mom said, but I refused to notice their brilliance.

The therapy was still going very slowly, and the dream of becoming a ballerina was moving further and further away. When school ended, I was glad not to be busy. I moped around the house and waited for the time to go to bed. Each night I looked forward to falling asleep, hoping to dream. My dreams had always been magical. But I didn't dream anymore. I was angry at my dreams for abandoning me.

The summer passed and the trees proudly displayed their radiant red and gold foliage, but autumn's splendor brought no delight, and it used to be my favorite time of year. I was feeling awfully sorry for myself.

One Saturday in late September after a long night of tossing and turning, I woke up before the sun. Nothing had changed. The summer's warmth still lingering, I wandered out across the lawn to wait for daylight to arrive. A meteor shower graced the sky. I made a wish and rested my heavy heart in its brilliant light.

Cradled in the soft, moist grass, I fell asleep, and for the very first time since my accident I had a dream.

> *The magic of Tchaikovsky's music*
> *Wraps around a carousel of young dancers*
> *Holding a garland of roses arched over their heads.*

> *As the chain of children weave in and around*
> *Swaying their garlands gracefully,*
> *I see Danielle and Robert and Carolyn.*
> *Their eyes sparkle. Their faces glow.*

When the gray mist of early morning faded and the sun rose in the eastern sky, I opened my eyes. Autumn's grandeur welcomed me. Even the leaves of the overhanging maple rustled a welcoming melody.

I lay on the grass until the sun shed its full radiance. A red-breasted robin tugged an earthworm out of the ground and swooped up to feed her baby chick on a limb of the tall oak. I smiled as I watched the robin feeding her fledgling.

Isabella saw me. She understood. Dashing across the lawn, her eyes sparkling, she licked my face with her long pink tongue. The earthy scent of her morning kibble never smelled so sweet. I pressed her firm body tightly to my chest. "Isabella, we'll go for a walk after breakfast. Mrs. Warren's rose garden's still in bloom. I know you'll enjoy smelling every fragrant blossom."

As I walked back to the house with Monkey Face, her tail tightly curled, I picked a pink rose for Mom that was just opening its petals to greet the new day.

At breakfast, my voice rising with enthusiasm, I told Mom every detail of my dream. "Mom I'm going to stop by the dance studio this morning." Mom's eyes filled with tears.

Turning a New Page

It had been so long since I held my abandoned ballet slippers. I hugged them to my chest before tucking them in my tote. I loved how they felt and smelled.

When I started to run down the street into town, even autumn celebrated. The reddening leaves danced in the gentle breeze, and a sparrow sang a sweet melody before flying off to meet his friends.

Then I remembered Dr. Braun's warning, "No running for a while, Sarah." The day my ballerina dream began to be real was still a vivid memory. Reaching for my dream that day, I ran down the street, thrust open the red door, and bolted two by two up the long flight of stairs. Yet having to slow down after my accident wasn't so bad at all. When the sun grew strong, the beads of perspiration made me feel alive again.

I tried to remain calm when I saw the brass toe slippers shining golden on the red studio door, but I didn't see myself on pointe in a sparkling pink tutu anymore. My heart raced, tempting me to bolt up the long flight of stairs, but I heeded Dr. Braun's warning and took each step carefully. At the top of the stairs the sun reflecting on the large mirrored wall filled the studio with a welcoming glow, and the smell of hard work drifted in the air. I sighed. This was where I belonged.

Danielle and Carolyn were warming up at the barre. They ran to me and gave me great big hugs. Robert came over and shook my hand. He was so grown up. Yet everything seemed so much the same.

"OK, class, everyone to the barre." Miss Hanson's voice rang brightly. When she saw me, she ran over and wrapped me in her arms. "You look wonderful, Sarah. I'm so happy to see you."

"Thanks, Miss Hanson. I'd like to stay and watch the children today."

"Absolutely. I'd love to have you assist me, dear. Everyone to the barre, please."

Before sitting down at the mahogany piano, Ellen held me so close my ribs hurt. I was home. The old upright piano and the rhythmic clap of Miss H's hands never sounded so good.

When I touched Danielle's shoulder, "Remember keep your chin up, Danie." Danielle kissed my cheek.

"Bobby, your front leg should be higher when you leap. Good. Now try to straighten your leg." Robert just smiled.

At the end of the class, Miss Hanson placed her arm around my shoulders, "Sarah, please come back next Saturday. The children were so happy to see you. and you have so much to offer them."

I went every Saturday after that. Although my dream of becoming a "prima" ballerina had been shattered, there was still a place for me in the world of ballet.

"Keep your eye on a spot on the wall as you turn. Much better, Danielle."

"Carolyn, when you rise up in *relevé*, you should be on full pointe. Beautiful."

"Bobby, your front leg should still be higher when you leap. Good."

Guiding my young friends as they prepared for their fall recital filled me with joy.

The night before the recital I had a dream.

> *The curtain rises,*
> *And a golden globe sends*
> *A circle of light to the center of the stage.*

In this golden moment
Danielle and Robert and Carolyn
Express the glory of dance.

On opening night I was so proud of my young dancers. "Danie, you pirouetted as if "held up by angel's wings." Even sharing Dad's words sounded right.

"Thanks, Sarah.

"Carolyn, your relevés were perfectly on pointe."

"Thanks, Sarah?"

Robert looked up and waited. "Bobby, you leaped across the stage like a gazelle."

"I tried to remember what you told me, Sarah."

"Bravo, my friends. Bravo." My dream had become their dream now, and I was happy to share it with them.

The following summer I began to take ballet lessons again, nothing very strenuous at all, and the seed of becoming a ballet teacher as good as Miss Hanson began to grow.

In the fall I sat under the dappled shade of the kwanzan tree surrounded by a bounty of yellow chrysanthemums and started writing again. Mom was smiling all the time now.

"Sarah, let's have a barbecue and invite your friends."

"Sure, Dad."

"Sarah, you're young, only at the beginning of a dancing career. There's so much a girl with your imagination can do. Your mother tells me you're a talented writer. I'm sorry but I have to recommend that you give up becoming a ballerina." Although it wasn't easy to hear those words, Dr. Braun was right. I had a lot of healing to do and writing was a good place for me to be. Maybe it would be only for a while. I didn't know. But I applauded myself for taking this giant leap in growing up.

I always enjoyed creating stories. Even before I could read and write, I was making up stories as I ran across the lawn with my little monkey face pug.

"Izzie, you be the prince, and I'll be the princess."

I remember Tuesday was my favorite day to go to nursery school. On Tuesday Mrs. Monroe called us one by one to her desk and asked if we had a story to tell her. She wrote the stories word for word in our notebooks, which she called our creative journals.

One Sunday it rained all afternoon, and I decided to clean out my desk. When I found my creative journal in the bottom drawer, I learned so much about myself. On the cover I had drawn a bright yellow sun, a big red rose, and a little rabbit with long pink ears. As I began reading the journal, I was four years old and back in nursery school again.

"Sarah, do you have a story for me today?

"Yes, Mrs. Monroe. I saw Mrs. Warren's orange and black tommie cat. He had big green eyes and was hiding in the hosta. Suddenly he began crawling toward a little pink-eared rabbit with a big white fluffy tail. The rabbit was scared and ran away."

"Would you like to get your crayon box and draw a picture of the cat and the rabbit, Sarah?" The orange and black tommie I drew had big green eyes and the little rabbit had long pink ears and a white fluffy tail.

"What story do you have for me today, Sarah?"

"I have a story about a big blue tarantula, Mrs. Monroe." I remember Mom read me a story about a tarantula that sparked my imagination and all week I had been thinking about the story I would tell Mrs. Monroe.

"What would you like to call your story, Sarah?"

"How Sarah Got Her Big, Blue Tarantula."

"Tell me about the tarantula, Sarah."

"Once there was a girl named Sarah who wanted an unusual pet. She wanted a big, blue tarantula. She begged her mom and dad to let her have a pet, and her father gave her some money to buy a pet. Sarah went to the pet store and came back with a big, blue tarantula named Felix. But her parents said she couldn't have it, and they threw it in the garbage pail. Overnight it crawled out and went into Sarah's room and slept on her arm. When her mother and father saw the tarantula, they were afraid. They called the zoo. A man came and looked at the spider and saw that it wasn't poisonous. And that's how Sarah got to keep her big, blue tarantula."

"That's a wonderful story, Sarah."

That day I drew a big blue tarantula with purple feelers, eight green legs, and four bright pink spots on his head. I loved telling my stories in colors that were vibrant and bold. I loved looking at the colors in my crayon box. On rainy days I often sat on the floor with the box on my lap. Sometimes I would take out a color and move it next to another color to see how it looked. My favorite colors were pink, blue, and green.

"Sarah, can I use your orange and green crayon?"

"Sure, Gregory." Gregory liked to color, too. I remember he drew a purple cat with a long orange tail and yellow eyes.

"Sarah, what's your story today."

"Today I saw a silver butterfly with turquoise dots, Mrs. Monroe. It was fluttering its wings around a lavender crocus."

"Sarah, would you like to get your crayon box and draw a picture of the butterfly for me?"

"Yes, Mrs. Monroe." I remember I was very careful where I

placed the bright turquoise dots.

"Sarah, what story do you have for me today?"

"This morning was very cold, Mrs. Monroe, and my little pug didn't want to go out. She just sat on her red cushion by the window. In the afternoon when the sun came out, she ran around in the snow. The snow was all the way up to her tummy. All you could see were her big brown eyes and her little curly tail. She didn't stay out very long."

"Sarah's stories are always so vivid and so filled with color," Mrs. Monroe had told Mom one day when she came to pick me up.

In kindergarten Mom and I wrote stories together. Just a blank, white page in my notebook could spark my imagination. When I got older and wrote my stories on the computer, the idea always began in a notebook.

In second grade my story hung on the bulletin board outside my classroom the whole semester. I remember I hadn't paid attention to Dad's warning, "Sarah, don't touch the lawnmower. It's very hot." That experience blossomed into this simple tale.

A Modern Fairy Tale

I think I saw a troll yesterday under the patio table. If I saw a troll, I think it looked like this. It had black eyes and a green nose with a wart on it. It seemed to have dried up skin that was purple. Then something blurry jumped out at me. It was so fast I couldn't see it. Then it zoomed away very quickly. But it left something behind under the table. Guess what? It was a baby gremlin. It was green with little yellow beady eyes. Just when I was about to grab it with my hands, it leaped away into the forest. But it left green slimy foot prints. I touched them and my hand turned green. I was terrified. I went inside. Mom said to soak my hand in water. But it didn't work. The gremlin came back today and left purple foot prints. I touched them and my hand turned back to normal. The gremlin never came back again. But I knew it warned me not to touch things I don't know.

Looking through what I had written as a child motivated me. Maybe I should write stories for my young friends at the dance studio. Writing was always healing, and it would only be for a while, I thought. Once again, I applauded myself for taking this giant leap forward.

Nature also has a wonderful way of healing. One Sunday in late October I woke up feeling sad. Although I had tried to keep my dream of becoming a "prima" ballerina in a special place in my heart, I still longed to be dancing again. Isabella and I went out on the patio, and autumn knew what to do. The red and gold leaves dancing in the wind carried my sadness away.

In the afternoon Betsy and I went to see *The Firebird* ballet. Like autumn's splendor, the majestic bird, a magical feather, and good overcoming evil brought me to a wonderful place.

Ever since I can remember I loved Tchaikovsky's music. I had been falling asleep to the *Nutcracker* or *Sleeping Beauty* or *Swan Lake* since I was a little girl. But Stravinsky's *Firebird Suite* was different, a modern sound wrapped in a once upon a time fairy tale. The music and the dance and the old Russian folktale came together like best friends.

The curtain rises on the dark world of Kaschei, an evil sorcerer. Prince Ivan arrives at the demon's castle. The rumbling drums express great danger.

Suddenly the sky lights up and a fiery red bird sweeps across the stage and flutters and spins around a tree bearing golden apples. The music shimmers with violins.

Charmed by the Firebird's beauty, her eyes sparkling like jewels, the Prince captures the winged creature. In her struggle to escape, the Firebird jetés and twirls and arabesques, her whole body in harmony with the beautiful music, her arms quivering like a humming bird in mid-air.

In this moment I remember the words Aunt May underlined in *Apollo's Angels* --a dancer requires "self-awareness, clarity, and training," Mr. Balanchine said. I long for the discipline and rigorous training that empowered the Firebird's magnificent solo. Before my accident, I welcomed the hard work, and now I missed it so much.

"Betsy, look at the curve of her back and the fluttering of her arms," I whisper. "I can feel every movement she's making."

Betsy nods enthusiastically.

When the gentle-hearted prince sets the Firebird free, she gives him a magical plume in gratitude and beckons him to wave the feather whenever he needs her help. Then spreading her arms like eagle's wings, the mystical bird disappears into the night.

"Betsy, she's spectacular."

Alone in the darkness, Prince Ivan wanders through the sorcerer's garden. Hidden behind iron gates, thirteen princesses are held captive by the demon. As they dance in a circle to the haunting melody of a harp, their beauty lights up the dark night, and Prince Ivan falls in love with one of the maidens.

This moment is magical for me. I embrace the crystal-clear melody of the harp and suddenly I'm far, far away dancing the magnificent Rose Adagio again. Rising up on pointe, I feel my body moving in harmony with the beautiful music. Betsy sees the distant look in my eyes. She understands. She reaches over and touches my hand.

At dawn the maidens return to the sorcerer's palace. Prince Ivan breaks open the iron gates and follows them. A loud chord sounded by the whole orchestra jolts me back to reality. The evil sorcerer and his hoard of ghouls appear. The scene is frenetic. As the music grows loud and agitating, I send my cherished memory back to that quiet place reserved in my heart. My magical moment doesn't belong in this frenzied world.

The sorcerer is terrifying and grotesque. When Prince Ivan asks the fiend for the princess's hand in marriage, the demon is infuriated and begins to cast a spell that will turn Prince Ivan into stone. At this moment the Prince remembers the Firebird's plume and waves the fiery red feather over his head.

Shining in the light of the moon, the mystical bird soars across the stage in grands je-tés and leads the sorcerer's monsters in a satanic dance. The horns are loud and aggressive. Driven by the Firebird, the monsters dance in a frenzy until they collapse.

The Firebird then reveals the secret of the sorcerer's immortality to the Prince. His soul in the shape of an egg is preserved in a casket hidden under a tree.

Prince Ivan finds the casket and smashes the egg. **The sorcerer dies**, his monsters fall asleep to a woodwind lullaby, and all the maidens are set free.

The big brass celebrates this moment of glory. Prince Ivan marries the beautiful princess and lives happily ever after in that place where dreams live.

"Bravo. Bravo."

Dance and Writing Intertwine

I loved *The Firebird* ballet and honored the majestic bird in a story I wrote for my young friends at the dance studio. It was the first story I had written since my accident. My love for dance and writing intertwined in a grand pas de deux. My young friends loved my tale of a fiery red bird who sends blessings to everyone.

A Garden Village by the Sea

The snow moon lights up the night sky, and a mystical bird with fiery red wings soars through the air like a shooting star. On the coldest night of the year, her long-feathered tail sweeps over the chimneys sending blessings to everyone.

In this garden village bordering the deep waters of the Mediterranean, the majestic bird's blessings have made the soil rich. The flowers flourish, and the trees grow tall.

The village lies at the foot of an ancient volcano, and the children, hearty and healthy, climb the steep, rocky cliffs like nimble mountain goats. In summer they explore sea caves created by the crashing waves and search for chestnut-tailed cave swallows with brick-red heads. Surrounded by beautiful rock formations, they wade through the shallow waters watching green sea turtles and balloon fish as big as basketballs drift around the seagrass beds.

Harmony and love abound in this garden village. The colts and the calves, the bushy- tailed rabbits, and the puppies and the kittens play together in the fields. In spring and in summer they sleep side by side with the stars and the moon shining brightly over them.

For many, many years the firebird, as the villagers call her, has brought them happiness. Each year when the snow moon lights the night sky, the majestic bird returns with glowing red wings and a tuft of flaming red feathers crowning her head. As the beautiful firebird wings her way over the rooftops, floating fiery feathers through the air, all the limbs of every tree shine ruby red.

At twilight on the coldest night of the year, the villagers go out to watch the luminous feathers float by. Dressed in woolen hats and mufflers and mittens, the children are allowed to go with their parents to get an enchanted feather to put under their pillow. As the feathers drift through the air, never reaching the ground, the girls have learned to leap as high as ballerinas and the boys as high as jumping jack rabbits to catch a feather to bring home.

It is said that only the children who are good are able to catch the radiant feathers. But the firebird's blessing fills the children with love that lasts all through the year, and they all go home holding a magical plume tightly in their hands.

Returning to their beds, the children place the feather under their pillow. Then as the snow falls silently and the moon shines bright, each child has a wonderful dream.

> *A luminous feather*
> *As bright as a shooting star*
> *Dances in the wind,*
> *Forever in motion,*
> *Twisting and turning,*
> *Bringing LOVE to everyone.*

As dawn breaks, the children awaken, and good things happen. The winter turns mild, promising the arrival of spring. When spring comes, the flowers and the crops grow in abundance.

In summer the children return to exploring the sea caves, and when summer ends and autumn leaves fall and the cold makes the air clear and the wind sting their cheeks, they are not sad. They know the firebird will return when the full moon lights up the winter sky.

Then one night, the coldest night of the year, a fierce wind blows and a large falcon with powerful wings flies in the glow of the moon's bright light. From a great distance, the hunting bird sees the beautiful firebird dancing like the wind as she soars over the rooftops. Enchanted by her fiery beauty, the greedy falcon wants the majestic bird for his own.

Swooping down at great speed, the falcon grabs the firebird tightly in his talons. The gentle bird cannot breathe in the greedy bird's tight grasp and struggles to escape, but the beast of prey is strong.

Taking off into the wind with the firebird held tightly in his beak, the raptor soars over the giant cypress trees and into the clouds. The villagers watch in awe and are afraid. They are fearful that the bird of prey will devour their magical bird, but the falcon wants only to keep the scarlet beauty for his own. The villagers, their eyes filled with tears, watch the falcon and the firebird grow small in the sky.

Soon love and harmony vanish from the garden village by the sea. The children fight and call each other insulting names. The colts and the calves, and the puppies and the kittens bite and strike out at each other. Nothing in the village is right anymore. The land has become barren and the villagers are hungry all the time.

For many years the scarlet beauty remains captive high on a cliff in the falcon's nest. In all the seasons that follow, the fathers in the village go out into the forest to search for the beautiful firebird, hoping to bring love and harmony back to their village.

In spring they return with only a handful of wild violets, faded and wilted, and the children throw them to the ground and stomp on them. In summer they return with baskets of mushrooms, and the mothers see they are poisonous and throw them away. In fall they return with a handful of dead leaves. When the villagers put them into a pile and set them on fire, the smoke has a foul smell.

Many years pass and the falcon grows old and dies. Still radiant and unharmed by her captivity, the firebird wings her way through the air to spread her blessings across the land.

Then one night, the coldest night of the year, the fathers trudge through the deep snow. Beneath the canopy of blue lit by a full moon, a fiery glow soars above their heads and glimmering feathers blow through the air. The majestic bird has returned.

When each father comes home with a fiery feather in his hand, all the children dance and sing and the animals frolic in the barn. Then the puppies and the kittens and the colts and calves lie peacefully, and the children go to bed and put the fiery feather under their pillow and dream.

> *A luminous feather*
>
> *As bright as a shooting star*
>
> *Dances in the wind,*
>
> *Forever in motion,*
>
> *Twisting and turning,*
>
> *Binging Love to everyone*

In the morning they awaken to the chorus of songbirds, the sun shining brightly. Harmony and love abound once more in the garden village by the sea.

At the end of the story, my young friends stood up and cheered. "Would you like to draw me a picture of the firebird, dancers?" The following Saturday they each brought in a drawing of a bird with fiery red wings and a tuft of flaming red feathers on her head.

Every Saturday after that, the young dancers would greet me with "Are you going to read us a story today, Sarah?" When I waved the book that Mom gave me with a picture of the Sugar Plum Fairy and her prince on the cover, the children were excited. They loved all the stories I wrote for them.

My Muse

A column of autumn sunshine streamed through the kwanzan tree casting a golden light on Isabella. Deep into sleep with her head on my foot, her legs move forward and back, forward and back. She's going somewhere. She's on her way.

On the patio table my new notebook waited to be filled. The sun shining on its newness beckoning me. I removed my foot carefully. Isabella lifted her head and opened her eyes, then fell back to sleep quickly to return to her dream.

I opened my notebook. Isabella and the white pages glowing in the sun sparked my imagination, and very soon I had another story for my young friends at the dance studio. The tale began in the twilight of day as the leaves drifted down like amber and ruby jewels and quickly turned frightening when darkness descended.

Out Alone

In the golden glow of autumn, birds chatter in the shade of crimson leaves. Isabella lies on the patio listening to the sweet melodies, her leash safely attached to the garden chair. A tiny chipmunk scurrying into the pachysandra passes before her, almost touching the tip of her nose. Hoping to make friends, the little pug charges after the critter, and the hook on her leash slips off her harness. Poking her nose into the dense green foliage to search for the little guy, she wanders all the way down to the heavily trafficked road.

Without a moment's thought, the little pug dashes into the path of a passing car. The car screeches to a halt. The loud and strange noise frightens the little pug dreadfully. For several minutes she stands in front of Shane's house to catch her breath.

But her desire for adventure has been awakened. Maybe Shane will join me, she thinks. He knows his way around the neighborhood. Walking quickly to the back of the Labrador's house, Isabella looks for her best doggie friend, usually lying in the shade of the tall maple tree at the back of his yard. But Shane isn't there today. Like an astronaut on her first trip to the moon, Isabella has her heart set on an exciting journey, a journey out alone for the very first time, and so rather unwisely, she wanders off on her own.

Sniffing a tree or a blossom or a single green leaf, the little pug's unaware how far she's roaming. The sun's just beginning to paint the sky in brilliant bands of pink and orange. She lifts her head to watch the twilight glow. The long tree shadows stretching to the other side of the road send a warning that darkness will arrive soon, and the nightly chorus of crickets have already begun their chatter.

As the shrill clickety-clicks grow louder, Isabella lies on the ground like a monk in prayer. She's afraid of the crickets. She's afraid of the shadows. She has lost her desire for adventure.

The impending darkness and the mournful sound of the rustling leaves have no sympathy for the little pug, and she desperately longs for home. Her thoughts wander to the comfort and safety of her bed. She longs to curl up by Sarah's side, to enjoy a yummy tummy rub and a kiss on her brow.

Frightened and bewildered, she lifts her head prayerfully to gaze at the handful of stars in the quickly darkening sky, perhaps promising never to roam from home again. Then continuing down the road in a determined stride, she stops briefly to sniff a mimosa tree. The familiar scent raises her spirit.

Lifting her head to nose the air, she smells the fragrant aroma of Mrs. Warren's roses. She quickens her pace, but her friend who's usually tending her garden isn't there tonight.

Mrs. Warren's tabby poses like a sphinx at the end of the driveway, his coat of fur burnishing copper in the setting sun. Tiger looks straight into Isabella's eyes but doesn't move. His unwillingness to help the little pug is not unexpected. In the past the unfriendly feline always ignored Isabella as she walked by with Sarah.

Making no eye contact at all, Isabella passes the tomcat quickly. Tiger remains still, only the tip of his tail twitching.

As the chorus of crickets grows louder, the hair on the little pug's neck bristles. She picks up her pace, her head down, her tail hanging low.

Dusty, Ted Parker's friendly golden retriever, barks a welcoming greeting from behind his fence, but even the gentle dog frightens Isabella tonight. The little pug sits down to catch her breath. She's consumed by an overwhelming feeling of loneliness. Continuing sullenly down the road, her big brown eyes express fear.

As night hastens to arrive, the brilliant hues of the setting sun still linger and the golden rays strike Mrs. Tremont's shingled house on the corner. Mrs. Tremont's just folding her chair to go inside. Isabella runs towards the lady, a beacon in the quickly descending darkness. "Please help me get home. Please," her big brown eyes plead.

Mrs. Tremont doesn't understand. "Go home, Isabella. Sarah will be worried about you. I have to prepare dinner now," and she closes the door quickly behind her.

The darkness has already begun to erase the tree shadows, and the crickets' chatter grows louder. Isabella is very afraid.

Romulus and Remus, two pit bulls who live next to Mrs. Tremont, are out on their front lawn enjoying a frisky toss, chase, and catch with a boy not much older than Sarah. Their long, tapered tails never stop wagging.

Isabella remembers what Sarah's friend had said, "Pit Bulls have a bad reputation, but they're really loyal and loving and playful. My dad's thinking of adopting a bully from the Rescue Center."

The thought calms the little pug. But when she gets closer, the imposing muscular bodies and wide jaws of the lively dogs make them look pretty tough. They remind Isabella of Rex, an American bull dog that visited the Bakers last summer.

That day Rex just sat all afternoon under the birch at the back of the lawn with his big head leaning on his front paws. Having waited all afternoon to play with the unfriendly visitor, Isabella finally walked up to him just as pale stars came out of hiding. Immediately the bully stood up and stared her down.

Rex had no intention of making friends with Isabella.

With that thought in mind, the little pug walks quickly passed the playful pitties. Engaged in their vigorous game of fetch, they don't notice her at all.

The autumn twilight's no longer there to comfort her, and the night air is beginning to turn cold. Her only hope is the white shingled house across the road. But Mugsy, Joe Raynor's pug, stands firm at the door of the white house. His surly tough guy face warns Isabella he surely will be no help. Defending his property fiercely, "Grrrrr. Grrrrr," Mugsy makes his feelings quite clear.

That's certainly a **pug**nacious pug, Isabella thinks. Her gentle, good nature finds it difficult to understand why Mugsy's always so ferocious.

Feeling really glum, she does what any frightened pug would do. She curls up under a rhododendron bush, a recognizable scent from home. Closing her eyes, she returns in her dream to the long ago and far away.

> *Panting heavily, Isabella reaches the pagoda.*
> *Rising majestically to the sky,*
> *The sacred monument stands as tall as a giant redwood.*
> *On the rooftop, golden and bell-shaped,*
> *Sapphires and rubies and jade as green as emeralds,*
> *Radiate in the moon's glow.*

Turning her gaze to the sky,
The little pug sees the serene image of a Buddha
Carved in stone above the entrance to the pagoda.
Her eyes focus on the figure.
She feels strong.
She's no longer afraid.

Isabella awakens calm. She has found strength and comfort in her dream and welcomes the sound of a car pulling into the driveway next door. Dashing over, she hopes to find a friend.

"Hi, Isabella," Mr. Bridges calls out from the open car window. When he swings the door open, Isabella jumps up into his lap.

"Are you lost, little girl? Do you want me to take you home?"

Tilting her head, her eyes twinkle "yes." Mr. Bridges understands.

"Don't worry, pal. I'll take you home."

Placing Isabella next to him, Mr. Bridges puts his arm tightly around her. The little pug snuggles close and licks his hand. The wrinkles on her monkey face hardly noticeable at all.

When they pull into her driveway, the trees are barely visible in the blue haze of the moonless night. Mr. Bridges rings the bell with Isabella nestled in his arms.

"Oh, Iz, I'm so happy to see you." Sarah hugs Mr. Bridges and her cherished companion, perhaps a little too tightly and a little too long.

"Mom, Dad, Isabella's home."

The next day when I read the story to Mom and Dad, Isabella was curled up on my lap listening to every word. I could see in her eyes she had learned a forever lesson. In the weeks that followed Miss Isabella didn't even like sitting on the patio alone. I can just imagine the thoughts running through her head __ What if a chipmunk passes by. Would I scurry after the little creature and lose my way again? That thought must have frightened her a lot. In the evenings as she snuggled next to me in bed, her big brown eyes showed no fear, and the crickets' chatter didn't scare her at all. She knew she was safe in her home.

When I read the story to my young friends at the dance studio, I knew they learned a proper lesson as well - - **Never, never wander away from home alone.**

Home Sweet Home

No crate for Isabella. As the harvest moon in a star-studded sky brings the day to a close, Isabella curls up in her bed in the corner of my room. Gazing up at the kwanzan tree, shining silver in the moonlight, she falls asleep quickly. Soon her eyes move rapidly, and I imagine she has returned to that special place where her dreams live, the long ago, faraway home of her ancestors.

A golden-roofed palace glistens in the moonlight.
A pug presses her nose to an orchid, silvery-white.

Next to a tall oak that almost touches the sky,
A small wooden bridge crosses over a blue-green pond.

At dawn a pink lotus rises from the blue-green water
And opens its petals to salute the sun.

The little pug lies at the edge of the pond.

A fat toad leaps up and sits by her side.

The lotus, the pug, and the frog unite in the golden light.

Like the little pug of long ago and faraway, Isabella lived in harmony with her environment. In spring and summer and fall she pressed her nose gently to every fragrant blossom in our garden. With her friends big Shane, lively Ted, and tiny Ariel, she romped in the lush beds of pachysandra that thrived all year. We took long walks together in all seasons, but when the air grew cold and the wind started howling, she liked sitting on her cushioned chair by the window watching the trees blow. That was Isabella's "Home Sweet Home," the place she loved most in the world.

One chilly, rainy day with Miss Iz lying cozy and warm by my side, I opened my notebook and began to write another tale for my young friends at the dance studio.

My Stay-at-Home Pug

It was the sixth of July, sunny and warm, when Isabella only ten weeks old arrived on the north shore of Long Island to live with Sarah and her mom and her dad. From the very beginning the little curly-tailed pug with a W of wrinkles on her forehead loved the Bakers and all her animal friends, especially Big Shane, the Labrador who lived across the road. But she loved Sarah most of all. Often you could find her curled up like a football on Sarah's lap or lying on the floor, her eyes barely open and her head on Sarah's foot. She loved snuggling in bed with Sarah, and they took long walks together.

"Come on, Monkey Face, let's go for a walk."

Isabella celebrated the natural beauty around her in all the seasons, and Sarah enjoyed watching her little pug sniffing a peony or a fragrant rose or a bright yellow chrysanthemum. In winter, her favorite time of year to stay indoors and cuddle, Sarah read her stories, wonderful stories about the enchanting world of fairies and all things magical. Sarah and her cherished companion were very good friends.

But today the little pug's life is going to change. For the very first time the Bakers are boarding Isabella at Katie's Place while they go on vacation. Not even the late morning sun can persuade the little pug to open her eyes this morning. Isabella refuses to leave her bed.

"Good morning, Monkey Face. "Go and eat your yum, yum." The tummy rub doesn't work, and the aroma of roast chicken hasn't tempted her at all.

"Yum, yum, Iz."

Isabella walks slowly over to her bowl, her tail between her legs and her eyes following Mrs. Baker carrying her bed and her favorite bowl and her special stuffed monkey Max to the car. A quick nibble and back to her bed, she tucks her head deep into the cushion to block out all the unpleasant sights and sounds around her.

"It's time to go, little girl. We don't want to keep Katie waiting." Isabella pretends she doesn't hear Mrs. Baker. Picking her up brusquely, Mrs. Baker carries the little pug to the station wagon and places her in the back seat. Sarah jumps in next to her and gives her a hug. "You'll be OK, Iz."

On the short drive to Katie's Place, the agitated little pug leaps up and down from the back seat to the front and back again.

"Please be a good girl, Monkey Face." Sarah holds her firmly in her arms and kisses Isabella's deeply furrowed brow.

When the car stops in front of a complex of apartments, Isabella stands firm in her leg- locked position and refuses to get out of the car. She certainly could be stubborn sometimes.

A woman walking her dog sees her resisting. "Oh, she's going to just love it here. There are so many dogs in the neighborhood. She'll have lots of friends."

Isabella furrows her brow. The pack of dogs she imagines greater in size than a lion or a bear roaming through her head are not comforting her right now. Anxious to get away from the lady with the bad news, the 15 lb pug jumps out of the car and surges across the courtyard like a huskie pulling a sled over the snowy plains in an Iditarod. Sarah struggles to keep up with her.

At the end of the courtyard, Isabella comes to a sudden halt at the staircase leading to Katie's apartment. She's lived all her life on one floor, and the steps have her very confused.

"You can do it, Monkey Face. You're a big girl."

With a sidelong glance that looks more like a scowl, Isabella struggles up the steps, losing her footing only once. The first of many challenges ahead.

The yelps and barks coming from Katie's apartment have her hair standing straight up. Since she was ten weeks old, she's lived a pampered life with the Bakers, surrounded by the sound of chirping birds and rustling leaves.

A young woman opens the door and holds Isabella's face in her hands. "Don't be afraid, little girl, my guys won't hurt you." With three energetic shih tzus running around like a brood of ruffians, the lady's gentle voice does not reassure Isabella. She's terrified to enter the apartment. The wild dogs with massive hairy manes look like little "lions." Even their sharp, shrill yelps, which might as well be roars, are disturbing. The little pug cowers on the floor and covers her ears.

"Dylan, Derby, Dublin, be good," the nice lady calls out and introduces the boys as her three d-linquents. Isabella's not amused.

Unruffled by the ruckus, a white cat sits quietly on the window sill, and a small brown poodle lying under the table in front of the couch ignores the tumultuous scene.

A man with a black beard is sitting on the couch smiling as he watches the melee. In a not very graceful leap to escape the wild ones, Isabella jumps up on the couch to get as close to the bearded one as possible.

Katie's husband Jim puts his arm around the whimpering pug and gently strokes her back. A good moment for Sarah to dash out the door before she begins to cry. "See you soon, Monkey Face. Be a Good girl."

Mrs. Baker's upset, too. Giving the little pug a hasty hug, she runs out, nervously slamming the door behind her.

In the car Sarah begins to cry. "Mom, do you think Isabella will be all right?"

She'll be just fine. She knows we'll be back to get her soon, and I gave her Max to cuddle."

But Isabella isn't fine. She lies by the closed door whining all afternoon. Time passes slowly, and nature provides no comfort. As the setting sun closes the day with a ribbon of pink, Isabella waits at the door for that magical moment when the Bakers will return.

"Cuckoo. Cuckoo." The kitchen clock announces dinner, and Katie serves the party of six. The white feline dines alone, and Timmy just lingers over his kibble. He's not feeling well. But Dylan, the bold one, stands proudly over Isabella's bowl, his full and glorious mane serving as a crown. Dismissing the manners he inherited from his royal ancestors, the little lion acts like the King of the Jungle tonight. Chomping like a wild beast devouring his prey, he gobbles up all the roast chicken Mrs. Baker sent with Isabella. The name little 'lion" suits him this evening. Long ago the ancients believed that shih tzus, the emperors' cherished companions, could change into a full-sized lion when danger approached.

Today there's no real danger. Isabella watches fearfully from a safe distance curled up in her bed. She's not hungry at all.

"Come on guys, let's go for a walk on the beach." Even Jim's deep voice frightens Isabella tonight, but when the three D's line up at the door, she's right at their tail hoping the night air will clear her head.

Unlike her quiet strolls with Sarah, walking with the three D's is more like racing across the plains of the Serengeti. As they dash along at an energetic pace making silly squealing and yelping noises, the three Ds are happy to share their nightly stroll with Isabella. But the little pug doesn't understand. Poor Isabella.

The moist sand oozing softly over her paws is cold, not like the light dew on the grass at home. She lifts her head to sniff the air. There's no fragrant scent of roses, only unfamiliar smells blowing in from the sea. Poor Isabella.

The small patch of grass shining in the moonlight raises her spirits. But when a spray of water from the breaking waves hits her face, she pulls back. There's nothing about this walk she's enjoying. Poor Isabella.

Back at the apartment she returns quickly to her bed, the only place that welcomes her tonight. The memories of bedtime stories and Sarah's goodnight hugs run through her head. She finally falls asleep and revisits a dream she had when she began life at the Canine Corners.

On a high hill
A golden-roofed palace glimmers.
Nestled in her bed in the King's chamber,
The little pug knows she is safe.
Suddenly a howl echoes over the hill.
Leaping to the window,
She sees a beast
In the light of a full moon.
A tattered flag in the distance
Flutters in a gentle breeze.

On the banner a horse bears a flame
Carrying blessings to everyone.
The little pug is not afraid.

"Cuckoo. Cuckoo." The clock on the kitchen wall strikes 10 AM. Warmed by the morning sun and the familiar aroma of roast chicken, Isabella opens her eyes. Emboldened by her dream, she's not frightened this morning.

Dylan, the bold has his hairy mane over her bowl of kibble. Derby and Dublin are right behind waiting their turn to get a piece of her roast chicken. Isabella stares Dylan down. Like a defeated king of the jungle, the bold one beckons his lion pride to follow him, and the three D's take shelter under the table where Timmy has been sleeping.

"I guess the little lions aren't so tough after all." Isabella struts triumphantly to her bowl.

Awakened by the thump of the three hairy ones by his side, Timmy stands up and follows the pleasant aroma of roast chicken. Isabella lets the poodle eat as much as he wants because he isn't feeling very well.

An uneventful day follows. Isabella stays most of the morning in her bed, but she's no longer afraid. She just misses Sarah so much.

At dinner when the three D's and Isabella and even little

Timmy gather at their bowls, everyone remembers his manners. Of course, the white feline with an imperial air always dines alone. Although Isabella never learns her name, she comes to think of her as Queen Liz.

After dinner she and the boys go for another roller derby run on the beach. This time Isabella takes the lead.

On the third day looking like balls of fire with their silky coats of fur shining violet and orange in the setting sun, the three little lions skillfully dodge the sea shells as they run and fetch the ball Jim tosses. Dylan's high-pitched bark beckons Isabella to join in the fun. Longing to play her favorite game, she takes up the chase. And like a spring rosebud that has started to bloom, a friendship between Isabella and the boys begins to blossom.

The next night Isabella leaves her cozy bed from home and joins the gang on Katie's bed. Ready to end the day with pleasant dreams, Dylan, the bold tries to get next to Isabella, but Timmy has gotten there first. Queen Liz, of course, sleeps alone on the couch.

The days go by quickly. Isabella has to admit that the toss, chase, and catch at twilight and the delightful romps in the tall grass and sand reeds are fun. The moist sand beneath her feet doesn't bother her anymore, and she's even getting used to the strange smells from the sea.

When Sarah and her mom come to pick up her up, they meet Katie in the courtyard holding two packages of roast chicken. "Your little girl has all the boys spoiled. They're acting like princes and want to dine on roast chicken every night.

Sarah laughs. Her mom smiles. "That's our little princess, all right."

Alerted by her family's voices, Isabella leaps over Dylan just as the door opens. Her tail in a tight curl, she gives long generous lollypop licks leaping back and forth from Sarah to Mrs. Baker. It was too hard to choose.

On the drive home she snuggles on Sarah's lap and quickly falls asleep. I'm sure she's dreaming of being back in her room with the sound of the chirping birds and the rustling leaves. Her adventure from home has been fun, and she might even visit her new friends again someday, but she's really a bona fide stay-at-home pug. Hugs and tummy-rubs and long walks lingering to sniff the peonies in springtime, the fragrant roses in summer, and falls bounty of bright yellow chrysanthemums suit her just fine.

Saturdays became my favorite day to go to the dance studio. After my lesson, I loved reading my stories to my young friends.

"Are you going to read us a story today, Sarah?" My Stay-at-Home Pug became one of the stories they never tired of hearing. "Sarah, read My Stay-at-Home Pug again."

Remembering

The snow fell silently on the night Isabella passed peacefully at thirteen years old. The only sound was the windchime swaying on a branch of the kwanzan tree. That year spring arrived early to comfort me. It rained gently and steadily in April and May. The light showers treated the new grass and rhododendron blossoms with care. The tulips and daffodils raised their heads to drink the nourishing mist, and every rose bud wore a delicate drop of dew.

One Sunday afternoon as I water the daffodils dancing in the spring breeze, I see Isabella in the distance. She appears like a dream. Mindful of the natural beauty around her, she's pressing her nose to a single wood-violet, her coat shining golden in the sun. She looks over to me, her big brown eyes sparkling, and dashes across the lawn. I can feel her bounty of lollypop kisses. Each luscious lick reminding me of the special bond we had.

"I loved your compassion, your love of nature, and your generous spirit, Isabella Ballerina. Thank you for being my very best friend and my favorite dancing partner," I whisper to the wind.

Keeping Isabella's memory alive is not difficult at all. She touched my life and so many others. I remember the summer her curiosity made a lasting impression on Mom and Dad and Mr. John. Spring had also arrived early that year. Red tulips sprang up everywhere, and the little rabbit with pink velvety ears had returned to munch on the new green golden in the sun.

I can still see Dad standing in the middle of the lawn clapping his hands loudly to scare the blackbirds foraging on the newly planted seeds. "Alice, it's time to fix the patio. The barbecue season will be here soon."

Mr. John the handyman arrived early the next morning, and Isabella sat on her cushion chair by the window to watch all day, jumping down often to whimper at the back door hoping to join him. "Not today, Isabella. You can't go on the patio while Mr. John is working."

It was nearly dark when Mr. John entered the kitchen, his hands covered in grimy grey dust. As he packed his tools, he called out, "If you find a brown leather glove, Mrs. Baker, just put it with my stuff in the garage. See you tomorrow, and don't step on the patio," his voice echoing down the hall. **"The cement is still wet."** Words of warning Isabella didn't heed.

Before Mr. John's car was even out of the driveway, Isabella pawed the back door open and dashed out to the patio. Sniffing here and there and everywhere, the choreographed pattern of her paw prints could have been on display in the Museum of Modern Art. But Mom and Dad were not impressed.

The next morning, sunny and warm, turned dark very quickly. Mom's voice resonated through the house. "Why, **why** did you do that, young lady? Didn't I tell you not to go on the patio?"

When Mr. John arrived, he shook his head in dismay, his voice rising, "You've been a bad girl, a very bad girl." Isabella, her head hanging low, tried to lick Mr. John's hand, but he just shooed her away. "Go away, bad girl."

Her tail hanging low, Miss Iz raced into the TV room and scratched furiously under the couch. Pulling out an object still covered in grey dust that she had hidden for a nice afternoon chew, she dropped it like a peace offering at Mr. John's feet.

"Isabella, you found my glove." Isabella's tail curled up, and she had that special twinkle in her eyes. Mr. John gave her a hug, and they were friends again. It was hard to be angry with Miss Iz for very long.

The memory makes me smile. I always knew the limelight suited Isabella Ballerina. Now like a movie star who leaves her prints on the Hollywood walk of fame, Isabella's paw prints left a lasting impression on the patio and Mr. John and Mom and Dad and me. She was our little star. She was so special.

I remember when we took her back to the Canine Corners for her first check-up. That day she showed us just how special she was. Unhappy to be in a portable crate in the back of the station wagon, she whimpered softly. Nothing of course as loud as a bark. She was too well-bred for that. Her heritage going all the way back to the emperors in the long ago and faraway.

As the Mozart Concerto filled the car, I opened the crate door. My little pug sprang into my lap and lay quietly listening to the music until she fell asleep.

Music was always important to Isabella. At bedtime when I played my CD of the beautiful Dance of the Sugar Plum or Rose Adagio, Isabella Ballerina always snuggled up in bed beside me and soon fell asleep, returning to that special place where her dreams lived.

> *In the early morning,*
> *The fragrant aroma of roses fills the air.*
> *A little pug mingles with the scent.*
> *In this simple moment*

The pug and the roses
And the golden light are one.

And the memories keep coming. I remember Miss Isabella had a great big appetite for a little girl. She loved almost everything Mom cooked, except for the disagreeable BEAN.

"Yum. Yum, Iz." When I offered her a lima bean or a kidney bean or even a great northern white, Isabella sniffed the tasty morsel, furrowed her brow, and whipped her head aside to get away from the unpleasant foe. I suppose she was just following a tradition of royalty because her head never turned away from a succulent piece of roast lamb.

Sometimes I gave her a strand of spaghetti, and she just swished it slowly into her mouth, never gobbling it down like some dogs would. Her good manners having been inherited from her royal ancestors.

One summer day when the fresh corn from the farm was served, I broke a cob in half and held it for her. She worked her way across the kernels like she was playing a harmonic. It was so much fun to watch.

When I miss my little pug, these memories are always there ready to raise my spirits. I often see her romping in the pachysandra that bordered our lawn, for her size equal to the Great Lawn in Central Park or the emperor's royal garden in the long ago, faraway land of her dreams.

I love you, Isabella. You were my cherished companion, my pampered princess, and my favorite pas de deux partner.

The moon's shines bright and a silvery glow dusts the lawn. I feel Isabella's presence tonight. In the glint of the moon's light on the window pane, I see her little monkey face. She's always going to be with me. I sit at my desk and begin to write a celebration of who she was. My little pug with a curly tail and a w of wrinkles on her forehead was so special.

My Little Pug's Way

As the morning star rises, Isabella lies beneath the kwanzan tree listening to the sparrows trill their song. Shafts of sunlight dapple her fawn coat gold and brighten her big, dark eyes. In this golden moment, surrounded by the sound and smells of a new day, she's in harmony with everything around her.

Two ants dragging a piece of a leaf many times their size cross in front of her. When the ants almost touch her nose, Isabella doesn't poke them, even in play. The gentle-natured pug tilts her head to watch them as they go on their way.

When the sun's rays become strong, Shane, a Labrador retriever and Isabella's best doggie friend, bounds across the lawn and lowers his head to touch the tip of the little pug's nose, their familiar doggie-kiss greeting. The rustle of leaves resounds through the air as the big dog and the little pug frolic in the pachysandra. Then Miss Iz and her friend walk side by side to rest in the shade under the kwanzan tree before Shane goes home.

Timmy visits with his master in the late afternoon. The poodle doesn't feel very well and curls up under the patio table. Paw-poking her friend gently, Isabella encourages Timmy to take a walk. As they stop to smell the roses, the sparkle in Timmy's eyes returns, and Isabella is filled with the joy that comes from helping a friend.

When Ariel, Isabella's cute little feline friend with big green eyes, strolls by, the sun is just beginning to set. Purple-blue irises circle the tall birch at the back of the lawn. The kitten and the dog roam freely around the tree. Surrounded by the fragrant aroma, the little pug and the feline and the blossoms are one under the rosy-pink sunset sky.

A finch alights on a branch of the birch. Isabella tilts her head to listen to the sweet song. Ariel stops to listen, her big green eyes gleaming. She has learned so much from her curly-tailed friend.

Teddy squeezes through the broken fence and pounces on Isabella. The little pug is happy to see her lively friend. When an ant carrying a leaf many times its size passes right before

Teddy's nose, the spaniel doesn't bother the ant. Isabella has taught Teddy to treat all creatures with care.

The sky has grown dark when Derby, Dublin, and Dylan, the bold come to visit, their hairy coats of fur shining silver in the moonlight. Isabella's happy to see the little "lion" dogs. They have become good friends.

"Come on, guys." Sarah calls Isabella and the boys to a frisky toss, chase, and catch. The little pug and the wild ones gather on the wide-spreading lawn under the canopy of stars. In this moment of fun, Isabella and the three D's barks and yelps mingle with the hundreds of crickets clickety clicking. Everyone is in harmony with the environment tonight.

When the shih tzus go home, Isabella lies on the cool moist grass to listen to the mockingbird sing. Lying on her back, she barks softly to get Sarah's attention. Sarah comes over and rubs her tummy. Cradling the little pug's face gently in her hands, she kisses her wrinkled brow. Sarah and her cherished friend and the mockingbird's song are one in the silvery light of the moon.

A hawk soars across the sky hastening to its nest. Sleep beckons. With the moon lighting the way, Isabella strolls across the lawn, lingering to sniff a rose before she curls up in her bed to return in her dreams to the long ago and far away.

A bed of wood volets covers the ground
Of a forest of tall oak trees
Reaching for the sky.

Narrow strips of sun stream through
The jagged green leaves
Ribboning Isabella's coat of fur.

Wending her way
Around the deeply grooved tree trunks
The little pug sniffs each purple bloom.

"Hugs and kisses, little girl. You played a major role in my life. Like the serendipitous moment I stepped into Miss Hanson's Dance Studio, you changed my life. You're my muse, Isabella Ballerina. You put my life back on track and helped me find my new dream."

Dreaming Our Separate Dreams

As I waited for the daisies to flower, I nodded to the lovely pink peonies, the first summer blossoms to arrive. Like the peony, the dreams that my friends had sown when they were four or five years old were beginning to bloom now.

From our very first playdate in the park, Patty and I had locked hands as we ran to the swings. When I swung from the highest rung of the monkey bar, she always stood by ready to catch me if I fell. "Sarah, be careful. You might get hurt." After my dancing accident Patty visited me every day. Her eyes were sad as she placed great puffs of freshly cut lilacs from her garden on my lap. Patty was such a good friend. She always had so much compassion.

Now I often see her walking slowly down the road beneath an early moon in her pink and white stripped uniform. Even long hours volunteering at the Shoreland Hospital haven't dimmed the sparkle in her eyes. She wants to be a nurse like her mom, and I know she's going to be a very good one.

Barbara's soft ball and bat have been thrown in a trunk with her other childhood toys. Now framed certificates of merit for her work at the Little Shelter and Animal Rescue Center cover the walls of her room. I always smile when I remember the day that she told us about the hyenas she saw on TV snuggling in their trainer's arms. "But hyenas are dangerous predators," I had said. "Not if they're loved from birth," she answered. "Animals are great and I love them all."

Now when we sit on the patio, her face radiant in the setting sun, she shares her day at the Rescue Center with me. "Remember the shy Labrador found under the porch of the empty house on the corner of Maple Leaf Lane? The vet said he was about 12 years old. Would you believe an elderly woman came into the center looking for a senior dog today? When she saw the Labrador, it was love at first sight. She took a pink ribbon from her pocket, tied it around the Labrador's neck, and left in a brisk stride with the big dog by her side. She even forgot her cane, but I don't think she'll be needing it for a while anyway." Every adoption made Barbara happy. She wanted more than anything to be a veterinarian.

Aunt May's dream and my dream have become Betsy's dream now, and we have become very close friends. Every fall we sit on the patio under the canopy of russet kwanzan leaves and choose a ballet to attend. *Swan Lake* was so special.

I remember sitting at the kitchen window on the morning of the ballet. December's cold frosting the pane didn't cover the memory of my shattered dream, and the mournful sound of the wind made me sad. But my love for the beautiful art of ballet has grown strong, and my heart expands with each ballet I attend. That day the glorious *Swan Lake* performed its magic.

The atmosphere in the auditorium was festive. Garlands of evergreens with big red bows were everywhere, but still my melancholy lingered.

The curtain opens on a moonlit night. A prince wanders alone by an enchanting lake where white swans float gently across the surface. As dusk falls a swan rises from the blue-green water and turns into a beautiful woman. When the lovely Odette dances, her movements so fluid, so dynamic, so elegant, all at once I want more than anything to be that ballerina again. Then I think about the beauty of her pirouettes, the curve of her head, the graceful movement of her arms, and I'm grateful for my understanding and appreciation of this magnificent art. I'll always have that. Ballet has shaped who I am.

I go to all Betsy's performances. In the winter recital she danced the role of Dewdrop in *The Waltz of the Flowers*. Moving between and around the waltzing flowers in a flurry of balancés and pirouettes, she danced beautifully. She was living my dream.

In the spring when the crocuses lifted their purple and yellow heads promising that winter would pass, Betsy bound into my room in a graceful jeté and announced, "Sarah, I've been accepted into the New York School of Ballet next fall." I know she's going to be a great dancer someday.

Sometimes what happens is the good stuff after all. When I enrolled in a summer writing workshop at the end of my senior year in high school, my new dream of becoming a writer began.

Outside the classroom window a Japanese maple tree glowed, its golden-green leaves translucent in the sun. Mr. Ford sat on the sill surrounded by the warm glow, his long legs stretching out, the familiar scent of Old Spice lingering in the air. "Greek mythology concerns the origin and nature of the world in which the Greeks lived. Throughout the ages, poets and playwrights, prose writers and artist have turned to myths for inspiration. Class, I would like each of you to create a myth or a fable that has significance in today's world."

That day Mr. Ford's assignment brought me back to the time when *Aesop's Fables* and *Sleeping Beauty* and the timeless fairy tales I read were my inspiration. A time when my imagination had no boundary. I looked through the notebook I kept with ideas for stories I had hoped to write. I chose the folklore legend of an ape-like creature that inhabited forests across the world.

Long Ago and Far Away

In a sheep skin tent at the foot of a high mountain, a little pug lies in front of a hearth,her head snuggled in a big dog's coat of fur. Outside the wind is harsh.

Around the fire children have gathered to listen to their father tell them the story of a giant ape-like creature. The tale has captured the imagination of the canines. They prick their ears up to listen.

"For many centuries an ape-like creature has roamed alone in this land of endless snow," their father says. "The beast has been seen walking upright with ease. Sometimes the creature leaves trails of blood that stain the snow red. No one really knows what living being left the blood. Some say it is the blood of a snow leopard or a bear or a tiger, the ape creature's prey." The little pug opens her eyes wide and tilts her head. Her eyes show fear.

"For hundreds of years men have followed the creature, and many have never returned," the father lowers his voice in a whisper. "Only in dreams has the beast ever been revealed to them."

As the burning embers glimmer and die, the little pug and the big dog nod off to sleep and dream of the mysterious creature.

> *In a cave at the foot of a high mountain*
> *A strange ape-like creature lives.*
>
> *With unflinching dark eyes,*
> *Hairy matted skin and sunken cheeks,*
> *The beast looks like a being*
> *Born when the world was young.*

In the morning the big dog leaps up. "Come on, Izzie, let's go and find the beast." The little dog follows her friend across the frozen plain and up into the mountains. Heavy flakes of snow whip across her face, burning her eyes and blurring her vision. She struggles to keep up with the Labrador. The big dog tries to stay at the little pug's side.

For miles and miles, the big dog and the little dog climb up the steep mountain. The way of life in this land of endless snow is not natural to the little pug.

Suddenly in the distance she sees a dark shape. The figure disappears, and a strange sound, almost like a chant comes from an opening in the mountain.

"Come on, Izzie, let's see what's in the cave." Emboldened by her friend's courage, the little pug follows the Labrador.

As they enter the cave, chanting fills the cavernous space. The little pug is afraid. She cowers in the corner and buries her head in her paws.

Suddenly a strange ape-like creature appears at the far end of the chamber. With unflinching dark eyes, the creature stands tall in a hollow in the cave wall. Wrapped in a hairy matted blanket, its face sunken and thin, the creature bears no resemblance to any human the little pug and the big dog have ever seen.

The Labrador slinks up slowly toward the hairy figure and sniffs. Dashing back to his friend trembling in the corner, he whispers, "Izzie, we have found the ape creature."

The little dog quivers in fear, the hair on her neck standing straight up. Then the unexpected happens. The beast begins to speak. He speaks slowly. His voice is deep.

"Many years ago, a great plague spread across the land. Thousands of people died, and everyone was afraid. I traveled far over the snow-covered land and into the mountains to escape the disease. Taking shelter in this cave I found peace. My body and my soul healed. At the end of each day, I offered my chant of gratitude. That was the sound you heard when you entered the cave."

Then the creature speaks softly. "In the winter I never left the cave and many years passed. One night as I stood at the entrance looking up to the sky, I heard a wild puffing sound, "Ow, Ow, Ow." I was afraid. Never had I felt such fear. That night I had a dream.

> *High in the mountains*
> *A snow leopard*
> *Big faced with a wide and open mouth*
> *Looks at me.*
> *His eyes show fear.*

The hairy one walks to a rock shelf at the back of the chamber and picks up a parchment, brown and frayed with age. The creature unrolls the scroll slowly and holds it up for the big dog and the little pug to see. "When I woke up, I drew the snow leopard as he appeared in my dream. The wild cat did not look fierce. That night I heard the puffing sound again and left the cave to find the beast. I found the cat curled up in a snowdrift. He, too, was afraid.

The young leopard was beautiful. Dark rosettes and spots on his thick coat of fur shone silver in the moonlight. He was hungry, and I gave him food. I was no longer afraid.

That winter I returned each night to the snowdrift to feed the snow leopard. We remained friends through all the seasons until my beloved leopard died several years ago." He bowed his head and looked tenderly at the picture.

Then the hairy one beckoned the big dog and the little pug to his side. "You have journeyed far from home and you are afraid. Even as you stand before me and hear my voice, I see fear in the little one's eyes. I say to the little pug that she must learn to see herself in all living beings and not judge until she understands." The big dog and the little pug left the cave so much wiser.

One day on her walk around the nomad camp, the little pug saw a wild hairy thing greater in size than any animal she had ever seen. The creature roared like a lion and his howls echoed throughout the mountainside. The little pug was afraid.

In the distance a boy ran after the dog and tossed a ball. The big animal chased the ball and returned over and over again for more of the chase and the catch. The mastiff played gently with the boy, very much like the little pug played with the children in her tent. Then she remembers the wise man's words, "See yourself in all living beings and do not judge until you understand."

When the hairy animal comes toward the little pug, she is not afraid. The mastiff sniffs her ear and lies by her side. And like the wise man and the snow leopard, the pug and the mastiff remained friends for a very long time.

"Sarah, your fable is very interesting and well-written," Mr. Ford had said. "I'll be happy to look over any stories you write.

Have you thought about becoming a writer someday?"

I appreciated what Mr. Ford said and knew I had many more stories in my head. And there would always be a place in my imagination for ballet of course. On the eve of Christmas I tucked one of my poems in Mom's Christmas stocking. While I lay in bed waiting for the arrival of Christmas morning, I heard Mom reading the poem to Dad. Her voice choking as she read the lines,

> *In a moonlit park*
>
> *Accompanied by the music of Chopin,*
>
> *A white-clad sylph*
>
> *Sweeps across the meadow*
>
> *As if carried on a current of air.*

"Tom, I hope Sarah will be happy. Wanting to be a ballerina was her dream for so long."

"I'm sure she will, Alice. Sarah's work with Miss Hanson's students still fills her with joy, and she has enjoyed writing and telling stories since she was a little girl. I know she'll be happy."

With *Sleeping Beauty* playing softly on the CD that night, I was happy even as I fell asleep dreaming of a prince offering me a rose, my leg extended in an arabesque. Ballet has shaped the way I relate to the world and has filled my imagination with so many wonderful memories.

Every year, the wind biting and the forecast often snow,

Aunt May and I go to *The Nutcracker*. As we sit in our red velvet seats, the enchanting world of this marvelous ballet appears like a dream. When the sound of the celesta rings heavenly bells and the Sugar Plum Fairy sweeps across the stage, I shed a tear. Aunt May reaches over and holds my hand.

"Sarah, maybe you'll write a story someday about a girl who has a dream of becoming a ballerina," Aunt May had said when she gave me a lovely notebook with the painting of Degas's *Ballet at the Paris Opera* on the cover. That was before my accident, and I just put the book on the top of my bookcase.

One night, the moon at its fullest, I have a dream, the same dream I had when I was a little girl.

> *In a majestic pine forest*
> *Filled with candied sweets and crystal snowflakes,*
> *A little ballerina sweeps into view.*
> *Beneath trees with snow-rimmed limbs*
> *Glistening in the moonlight,*
> *She dances like the wind.*

In the morning I open the book. My memories and my imagination and the blank pages form an intimate relationship, and I begin to write *Where Dreams Live*. I don't want ever to lose the spirit of a child's imagination, and the dream coming tomorrow may be the best dream of all.

About the Author

As a young girl taking ballet lessons, Anne Dupré fell in love with the beautiful art of dance. Now a retired English professor living on Long Island, she has the opportunity to attend several ballets each year at Lincoln Center. These ballets and her memories come to life on the pages of *Where Dreams Live*.

She has published three books, *The Little Pug's Dreams*, *It's Time to Tell a Story*, and *The Brightest Star in the Sky*, filled with memorable experiences that have shaped her life.

www.ingramcontent.com/pod-product-compliance
Lightning Source LLC
Chambersburg PA
CBHW070940190726
48292CB00004B/1263